Panic was like a frantic caged bird beating against her breastbone as they drew closer

Rafael opened his door and turned and picked Isobel up in his arms so fast that her breath caught and she felt dizzy. "What are you doing?"

"Carrying you over the threshold." And he did just that, before putting her back on her feet on the other side.

His bed loomed large and threatening through the door of the bedroom just feet away. She put up a hand, panic strangling her voice. "Wait— stop," she blurted out. "I just… I really want to go to bed alone. This has all happened so fast. I've barely seen you since we came back to Argentina. Two weeks ago I was living in Paris, yet here I am…. It's a lot to take in."

Rafael just looked at her, his face unreadable in the shadows of the dark room. Eventually he let out a breath and ran a hand through his hair. Tension vibrated off him in waves, enveloping Isobel.

"I'm not in the habit of forcing unwilling women into my bed, Isobel, and I've no intention of starting now with my wife. Please, by all means, go to your own bed. But soon enough you'll be welcoming me with open arms."

All about the author...
Abby Green

ABBY GREEN deferred doing a social anthropology degree to work freelance as an assistant director in the film & TV industry—which is a social study in itself! Since then it's been early starts, long hours, mucky fields, ugly car parks and wet-weather gear—especially working in Ireland. She has no bona fide qualifications but could probably help negotiate a peace agreement between two warring countries after years of dealing with recalcitrant actors. Since discovering a guide to writing romance one day, she decided to capitalize on her longtime love for Harlequin® romances and attempt to follow in the footsteps of such authors as Kate Walker and Penny Jordan. She's enjoying the excuse to be paid to sit inside, away from the elements. She lives in Dublin and hopes that you will enjoy her stories. You can e-mail her at: abbygreen3@yahoo.co.uk.

Abby Green

BRIDE IN A GILDED CAGE

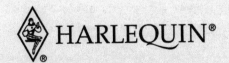

HARLEQUIN®

TORONTO • NEW YORK • LONDON
AMSTERDAM • PARIS • SYDNEY • HAMBURG
STOCKHOLM • ATHENS • TOKYO • MILAN • MADRID
PRAGUE • WARSAW • BUDAPEST • AUCKLAND

Recycling programs
for this product may
not exist in your area.

ISBN-13: 978-0-373-12948-5

BRIDE IN A GILDED CAGE

First North American Publication 2010.

BRIDE IN A GILDED CAGE

This is especially for Sinead O'Connor
(lovely friend), who brought me to
my first tango lesson, which infected me
with the tango bug.

This is also especially for Ann Murphy, who
enriches my life and my tango world on a
regular basis, with much thanks.

And, lastly but not leastly, this is for
tangueros and *tangueras* everywhere!

CHAPTER ONE

DON RAFAEL ORTEGA ROMERO looked at the girl standing across the room from him. He knew she would be no different from her social peers in their privileged circles in Buenos Aires: rich and spoilt. She was paler than her contemporaries, but he guessed that came from her English father. Her mother, Maria Fuentes de la Roja, was Argentinian aristocracy through and through. His brain felt slightly fuzzy around the edges and he cursed himself mentally; one shot too many of whisky wasn't going to help him out of this predicament, or the feeling of entrapment he'd lived with for years.

It was Isobel Miller's eighteenth birthday tonight, and he'd finally come to meet her face to face. Because this was the woman… He amended that now with a twist in his gut. This was the *girl* he'd been promised to in marriage since he was eighteen years old.

'You can't make me marry you!'

Isobel's chest rose up and down with her agitated breath. She'd never felt so threatened and intimidated in her life. Her hands were clenched into fists at her sides, and she felt frumpy and awkward in the too tight and fussy satin dress her mother had made her wear for her birthday celebrations that night.

The man across the room just looked at her coolly and said,

in a deep voice that sent a disturbing frisson of awareness through her, 'I'd like to say that your reluctance is refreshing, but I doubt you really mean that—especially when you know you have no choice in the matter. When your grandfather sold your family's *estancia* to my father, he rewrote your destiny.' His mouth thinned into a bitter line. 'They both got what they wanted—your grandfather got money from the sale with the assurance that the *estancia* would return to the family through you by walking away with a watertight marriage agreement.'

Isobel struggled to comprehend. 'You mean...you mean that your father was played? But that's—'

'Hardly.' He cut her off, his voice grim. 'My father didn't get *played* by anyone. He had a bone to pick with your grandfather and he was the only one willing to make an offer on a property too huge for many others to contemplate buying. But he made sure he got what he wanted in return—a dynastic marriage between his son—*me*—and someone from a suitably impressive lineage—*you*. Your family fortunes leave much to be desired at this time, but that is neither here nor there. Your family are still considered pillars of Buenos Aires society. Ten years ago, when the deal was done, your grandfather only received half of the *estancia*'s worth. My father, using his profession as a lawyer to best advantage, made sure that your family would only receive the other half on the day of our wedding—on your twenty-first birthday.'

Isobel reeled. She'd *known* about this since she'd turned sixteen, known that this day might come. But she'd pushed the prospect away, deep down where she wouldn't have to think about it, hoping that if she didn't acknowledge it, it wouldn't manifest itself. The thought of an arranged marriage to one of Buenos Aires's scions of industry had been too barbaric to contemplate, and going to secondary school in

England and living most of the time with her father's family there had helped cushion her from the truth.

But the reality was manifesting itself in front of her right now, mocking her paltry hopes that it might never happen. Panic clawed upwards through Isobel's throat, constricting it slightly. 'It's not *my* fault that my grandfather felt compelled to sell the *estancia* and broker such a deal.'

It was hard for her to cling onto any sense of reality right now. It had been hard enough to contemplate coming back to Buenos Aires after leaving school in England with the prospect of telling her parents she wanted to go to Europe to pursue her love for dancing. She'd always found the more conservative society of Buenos Aires constrictive—especially after spending time with her more relaxed and down-to-earth English relations, who would frequently debate around the dinner table. They hadn't known about her arranged marriage, and she'd never mentioned it to them, mortified at how medieval it would sound.

Her years of relative freedom in England had given Isobel an objective view of her privileged upbringing, and she knew with a passion that she could never slot into the life of a pampered millionaire's wife—which was what so many of her Buenos Aires girlfriends were doing, despite their own schooling in exclusive schools all around the world.

Don Rafael Ortega Romero gave a short sharp laugh now, making Isobel flinch minutely, and she felt her heart kick when she saw a flash of white teeth. 'Are you really that naive, little Isobel Miller? Our whole privileged society is based on unions of strategy and convenience. Marriages have been arranged for many, many generations. I'll give you that this particular one seems to be a little more arbitrary than most, but really it's no different.'

He smiled, and it was devastatingly cynical. 'If we all believed in true-love matches, the upper echelons would collapse into anarchy in the morning—and believe me, I've first-hand knowledge of that.'

In a slightly crumpled tuxedo, white shirt open and bow tie hanging rakishly undone, with a potent aura of raw sexuality surrounding him, the most elusive and sought-after bachelor in Buenos Aires was effortlessly living up to his arrogant and ruthless name. His hands were thrust deep into the pockets of his expertly tailored black trousers. Rafael Romero was a truly magnificent specimen of virile masculinity.

The threat of no escape and a forced marriage made Isobel's chest constrict with fear, but she felt a flash of fire in her belly and said through gritted teeth, 'I'm not *little* or naive, and it is positively medieval in this day and age to expect people to agree to an arranged marriage like this.'

Isobel had followed her parents into the hall earlier when he'd arrived. The front door had remained open momentarily, along with the back door of his chauffeur-driven car. Isobel had caught a glimpse of a long, sleek leg, a seductively high-heeled shoe, before his driver had shut the door on the view.

Looking at photos of this man in the press had done little to prepare Isobel for his effect on her face to face. His skin was a deep dark olive, his hair as black as midnight, and his eyes were like two pools of dark sin. His face was hard and uncompromising, with an almost cruel aspect that was soft-ened only by the most decadently sensual mouth she'd ever seen on a man—even when it was set in a grim line. She shook herself inwardly. She'd looked him up once on the Internet, with a sick fascination, and had read that his business methods had been praised and lambasted in equal measures for being cutthroat.

He was a rich playboy tycoon, used to riding roughshod over people. She had to stand up to him—make him see that she wouldn't just succumb like some sacrificial lamb.

He'd dismissed her fawning parents just moments before, with a curt, 'Leave us. I've come here tonight to speak to your daughter alone.'

She hitched up her chin now. 'Why did you come here tonight? I didn't invite you.'

His mouth quirked, mocking her attempt at bravado. 'You must have known that we'd meet sooner or later. Why do you think your parents insisted on your return from England?'

That panic surged back, gripping Isobel tight inside her belly. The fact that her mother hadn't even warned her that he was coming made her go cold inside. She must have anticipated how Isobel might react.

'We're not getting married,' she denied desperately.

He shrugged minutely, unconcerned. 'Not right now, no. But in three years' time we will become man and wife.'

The walls of her life were encroaching around Isobel. This was her worst fear: being marched into a life she had no control over, being forced into a marriage of convenience with someone she didn't love, and growing cynical and bitter just like her own parents. Her vision of a future in Europe, far away from here, was quickly crumbling.

She could feel the colour draining from her face. 'But I don't want to marry you. I don't even *know* you.' She looked at him then, feeling a little wild. 'I don't want this life. And I don't care if you believe me or not. I would be quite happy to walk away right now and never see you, or this house or Buenos Aires ever again.'

She gestured with a shaking hand, horror taking hold now, alongside her escalating panic at the thought of succumbing to a life with this cold man. 'How can you be so blasé about this? Coming here to meet your future wife when you're quite obviously in the middle of a date? Does that woman out there know that you're in here discussing your marriage?'

He smiled again, a hard smile, and drawled, 'A date? That's cute. The *date* you refer to took place earlier this evening, but I can assure you that the woman in my car will be perfectly happy once she's in my bed and underneath me. She doesn't care about marriage any more than I do. She's already been twice divorced.'

'You're disgusting.' And yet his words had sent another deeply betraying quiver of awareness through her body.

Rafael shook his head and came closer to Isobel. She stood her ground.

'No, not disgusting. Realistic. Two consenting adults coming together to enjoy one another without any of the bare-faced lies most lovers indulge in.' His eyes flicked Isobel up and down insultingly. 'When you become an adult you might appreciate that a little better than you do now. Clearly you haven't moved beyond slushy teen romances.'

Isobel had never felt so angry in all her life. Red spots danced before her eyes. 'It's a pity you never married the fiancée you were prepared to risk this union for. If you had, we wouldn't be discussing this now. Was it your charming cynicism that sent her packing?'

Isobel saw his face darken at her provocation, but she didn't care. She was referring to the fact that he'd ignored the legal agreement between their families to get engaged some eight years previously. Isobel had not known then of his significance in her future life, and she could remember looking at pictures of the gorgeous passionate couple, and thinking how impossibly romantic they had seemed.

But the engagement had died a quick death in a blaze of publicity. There hadn't even been time for Isobel's family's legal team to use the potential marriage as an excuse to get the money owed them from the *estancia*. As soon as the engagement was off, the agreement stood again. And then, when she'd turned sixteen, her parents had broken the news to her.

When she'd researched him, she'd looked up all the old press reports of Rafael's engagement to the stunningly beautiful Ana Perez, and for the first time, to her mortification, had realised that the reason for their break-up must have been *her*. Reports alluded to an arranged marriage but never revealed between whom. And since then his reputation with women had invariably been compared with how he dealt with his business concerns: merciless precision, no woman ever lasting longer than a few months.

'No,' Rafael said coldly now, more than a little stunned at how this girl before him was turning his preconceptions of her on their head. 'It's not a pity at all that my engagement didn't work out. It was a blessing in disguise. When *we* marry it'll be like any other business arrangement—which is exactly what a good marriage should be.'

He hadn't expected the words to come out so easily, but declaring to this girl that they would marry felt right on a level that disturbed him. His voice became harsh. 'There is no escaping this fate. I've learnt that, Isobel, and you will, too.'

Suddenly, in that instant, something undefinable solidified in Rafael's chest. A sense of inevitability. He'd come here tonight to meet for himself his bride-to-be. He'd come with his mistress in tow, which he knew was reprehensible, but it had made him feel somehow protected.

The fact was, he'd blocked out the reality of this marriage

successfully for years—until his solicitor, an old and trusted friend, had rung him earlier that day and said bluntly, 'It's Isobel Miller's eighteenth birthday today. Don't you think you should acknowledge the fact that her parents have been begging an audience for months now? This isn't going to go away, Rafael. You need to deal with it, *with her*, and the fact that you're not getting any younger. The longer you remain single, the more unstable you will appear in the eyes of your potential clients and colleagues.'

Rafael had muttered something rude, which his solicitor had wisely ignored. The minute he'd mentioned Isobel Miller something tight had formed in Rafael's chest—that sense of a trap closing around him. He wasn't used to being at the mercy of anything. And along with the feeling of entrapment had come the bitter reminder that his ex-fiancée had used that information to expose his one weakness for her own avaricious benefit.

His solicitor had cut in. 'Do you want to jeopardise the *estancia*? I've warned you before, Rafael, that if you try and get out of this marriage you'll embroil yourself in a huge and lengthy legal battle, and there's every chance you could lose. One of our advantages in this situation is that Isobel's parents seem loath to do battle, too, and that can only be because they need the money so badly.'

Curtly, Rafael had replied, 'Don't worry. I'm not about to risk losing one of my most valuable assets.' His lip had curled. 'Not for a woman.'

His solicitor had sighed audibly with relief. 'I knew you'd see it that way. Well, then, the sooner you can come to terms with this and meet your future bride the better. Her mother has extended to you an invitation to go to her birthday celebration tonight.'

He could have laughed now, though—Isobel Miller was the one woman who didn't even have to try and seduce him to get him to marry her! He was being served up to her on a plate, and here he stood, listening to her protest against what any other girl would have given her right arm for.

At that moment, in the tense atmosphere of the study, Isobel got a tiny glimpse of indefinable emotion in Rafael's eyes. When had he moved so close? She could see now that his eyes were a deep, dark brown, like molasses, with shifting glimmers of green and gold—not entirely black, as she'd thought.

Sensing some aspect of the man she might appeal to, she said, 'But you don't want to marry me. Can't you just give us what we're due for the *estancia* and we can be done with this arrangement?'

Before Rafael's very eyes Isobel Miller was changing. His first impression of her as a girl hadn't been entirely fair. She just looked incredibly young. But now he could see that she had an inherent maturity, a worldliness he wouldn't have expected. His eyes compelled hers to his, holding them. He shook his head. 'No, it's not that simple.'

Rafael found his thoughts scattering as he became increasingly transfixed by her. Up close, she was even paler than he'd first thought. Brown hair with a hint of russet shone in the dim light of the study. It was caught up in a fussy chignon that did nothing for her face, which still held some teenage plumpness. But her eyes…he found himself caught by them. They were huge and brown, like dark velvet, with long lashes casting shadows on flushed cheeks.

He could see in an instant that once her teenage plumpness disappeared she'd have the potential to emerge as a true beauty. Disturbingly, he felt a rush of blood to his groin.

Why was he just staring at her like that? Isobel spoke

again, with more than a hint of desperation in her voice. '*Why* is it not that simple?'

She was unaware of the hopelessly pleading look on her face, and didn't see how Rafael's jaw tightened in response. He took a step closer, and now Isobel felt even more threatened. Rafael Romero at a distance was truly intimidating, but close, like this, he was altogether overwhelming. She found it hard to breathe.

'I am not going to risk losing the *estancia* by trying to negotiate a way out of the agreement. And the fact is I will need a wife. Why would I turn my back on one so conveniently provided?'

His eyes dropped in a leisurely appraisal of Isobel's body, making her heat up so that her face felt brick-red by the time their eyes met again.

'You're not what I expected,' he said, almost musingly.

'Well, you're *exactly* what I expected,' Isobel threw back, feeling more and more threatened.

Rafael arched a brow. 'I'll take that as a compliment, shall I? You're quite the little firebrand, aren't you?'

Isobel hitched up her chin. 'If by that you mean I've got a mind of my own and I'm not afraid to use it then, yes, I am a firebrand. And if you think I'm going to meekly agree to a marriage of convenience with you then you're sorely mistaken. I've no desire to commit myself to a life of purgatory as some billionaire playboy's convenient wife.'

Isobel felt even hotter, and hoped the dim light was hiding her reaction. The way he was looking at her was so…assessing. Too assessing. As if he saw something that she'd never been aware of—herself as a woman. Immediately something liquid and illicit pooled in her belly and down lower. She fought not to squirm. She wanted to look away, anywhere but into those dark, hypnotic eyes, but she couldn't.

The futility of their circumstances washed over her. His enigmatic silence was sending her tension levels into orbit. 'You can't seriously tell me you're happy to marry me.'

His mouth was grim, hard. His eyes weren't assessing any more; they were hard and black. 'On the contrary, Isobel, I came here tonight to see my future bride for myself, expecting to meet a vacuous spoilt brat, but you've confounded my expectations—and, believe me, not many people surprise me these days.'

Isobel went cold inside. 'I don't want to confound your expectations.'

'Tough,' Rafael said easily. 'You have. I will admit that the prospect of this marriage has held little appeal for me, but my attitude is changing by the second. My eventual need to marry was never in doubt, and after my near-fatal brush with matrimony, let's just say that a marriage of convenience is the only type of marriage I'd contemplate.'

His gaze flicked down and up again, and his mouth softened, making Isobel quiver inwardly.

'While I've no desire to take a child bride into my bed, I can see that with a little more maturity you might well become a woman I can make a life with.'

Now Isobel was fierce, some innate feminine pride surging upwards, along with the sheer panic his words engendered. 'I'm *not* a child.'

Rafael arched a brow. 'No? Then what are you—a woman?' He shook his head and said cruelly, 'You're not a woman yet, *querida*, and you're certainly not ready for my bed.'

White-hot anger and something scarily like hurt made Isobel spit out, 'By all appearances your bed is far too busy anyway. I don't think I'd like to share it with every social climber in Buenos Aires.'

Rafael looked stunned for a moment, and then livid. 'Why, you little—' He reached out and put his hands on Isobel's arms, pulling her into his chest.

She couldn't gasp, couldn't breathe. Eyes opening wide, she saw Rafael's head descend and that unbelievably sensuous mouth come closer and closer. She let out a strangled gasp before everything went black and *hot* and Rafael's mouth closed over hers. He tasted of whisky and danger—an altogether intoxicatingly adult mix.

The boys she'd kissed in England could never have prepared her for this sensual onslaught.

Sheer shock kept Isobel immobilised for a long moment. Too long. Because suddenly all she was aware of was how hard Rafael's chest felt against hers, how it made her breasts tingle and swell against her dress.

His mouth was hard and ruthless, punishing her and expertly seeking a response so that he could humiliate her some more. Isobel knew in some distant part of her brain exactly what was happening, but that part of her brain seemed to be disconnected from her body and her mouth.

She found her hands clinging to the lapels of his jacket—clinging because her legs had turned to jelly. When Rafael's mouth moved away for one second Isobel heard a mewl of distress come from her throat as she blindly sought and found Rafael's mouth again.

His hands moved—one down her back, the other to the back of her head. She could feel him loosen her hair, so that it fell around her shoulders. Her world was reduced to delicious insanity. This man and his arms and his mouth on hers. So hot and demanding, like nothing she'd ever known or imagined. The touch and slide of his tongue against hers made her legs clench together to stop the pulse throbbing between them. Liquid heat was spreading outwards from the very core of her being…and Isobel had no hope of clawing back rationality or any pretence that Rafael wasn't blowing her mind to pieces. Her inexperience rendered her helpless.

He was the one to eventually pull back. Isobel opened heavy eyes, her breath coming hard and fast. Heart thumping. She felt hot and sweaty and desperately disorientated. As if her inner being had just shifted on some level and been reorganised. She felt as if he'd branded her.

Rafael carefully made sure she was standing, and then dropped his hands and moved back. Humiliation rose swiftly. Isobel couldn't look at him. Face burning, she sat in the chair beside her. She couldn't even pretend she was unaffected. It would be the most obvious lie in the world.

Rafael paced a few feet away, all his coiled energy reaching out and making Isobel want to curl up and hide.

He stopped pacing, and his voice had a rough edge that had Isobel's pulse skittering again. 'Like I said, you're not ready for me, Isobel. But in three years, when we're due to marry, I've no doubt you will be.'

He sounded almost surprised, and Isobel looked up—then wished she hadn't when she saw he was so close, looking down at her. Before she could escape he was reaching down and putting those big hands on her arms to lift her to her feet. She trembled all over.

He tipped up her chin with a finger, his eyes roving over her face as if he was inspecting her all over again. 'Marriage between us is inevitable, and I do believe that perhaps we can make a good one. We've got as good a chance as anyone in this city facing a marriage like this. Any reluctance I may have once felt is fading fast.'

He was talking as if she weren't even there, almost musing

to himself. Isobel stood stiffly and gathered all of her courage. 'I won't marry you.'

Grimly, Rafael's eyes caught Isobel's, and the force of rejection in his body at her words surprised him. 'You don't have a choice. Our futures are bound together. Like I said before, I've no intention of jeopardising my ownership of the *estancia*, not for anything—and certainly not for a convenient bride I intend to make full use of.'

His mouth twisted humourlessly. 'You should be counting yourself lucky that you have some time to get used to the prospect. When we do marry, Isobel, you will be my wife and by my side in every sense of the word.'

Hysteria rose within Isobel at the thought that he believed she would become the kind of woman he could marry. Never. The thought of living in Buenos Aires with the prospect of marriage to Rafael hanging over her head felt like a prison sentence.

She shook her head, felt the slip and slide of her hair over the sensitised skin of her shoulders. 'No. I'm going to leave. Get away from here. I won't marry you. I *won't*. I'd prefer to die.'

A cynical look crossed his face. 'No need to be so dramatic, Isobel. When we marry we'll simply be joining the thousands of others before us who've had to marry for convenience and inheritance.' His eyes flicked down and back up. 'With a little time you will mature into a woman I can take into my bed as my wife…'

Sheer hurt winded Isobel. She still hadn't fully processed the effect of that kiss, but Rafael had proved his sensual dominance over her with effortless ease. And her very obvious lack of effect on *him*.

The sheer threat of what Rafael said made Isobel forget everything rational, all the reasons why she didn't have much choice in this matter. 'I'm not scared of a legal agreement. It's not *my* fault that my grandfather was forced to sell the *estancia* to your family. I won't pay for his choices with a marriage of convenience to someone I despise.'

Her fists were clenched, nails scoring grooves in her palms.

Rafael stepped back, dropping his hands, and conversely that made her feel slightly bereft.

He smiled minutely, and that seemed to make the floor tilt underneath her. '*Despise* is a strong word when you barely know me, little one. Run away all you want, but I'll know exactly where you are and what you're doing—every single moment. You're a Buenos Aires princess, Isobel. Your life is here. You wouldn't survive for two minutes outside your protected environment in the real world. And I really wouldn't advise you to do anything rash like elope—either to escape your fate or for love…'

His voice turned bitter. 'I'll save you the heartache now. It wouldn't work out, and my team of lawyers would see to it that your family never sees the money they're due if you pull a stunt like that. It's a considerable amount of money, and I can guarantee you that your family's very survival in this society revolves around getting it—especially if their finances continue on the downward spiral they appear to be on.'

'I hate you,' Isobel said shakily. 'I hope I never lay eyes on you again.'

Rafael reached out and trailed a finger down Isobel's cheek. 'Oh, but you will, Isobel, you can count on that. We're going to have a long and happy life together in the not too distant future.'

CHAPTER TWO

Nearly three years later

THAT KISS... Rafael had given up trying to figure out why the kiss he'd shared with Isobel Miller that night had impacted upon him far more than he'd let on at the time. It still had an uncomfortable habit of sneaking into his thoughts with annoying and vivid frequency.

He could remember going back out to his car, where his mistress had been waiting, and dropping her home with some pathetic excuse—an unprecedented situation. But it hadn't just been the kiss that had turned his head, made him stop to think about the marriage in a new light. It had been the way she'd stood up to him—something no one before or since had done. It had made him believe that the prospect of their arranged marriage might not be the prison sentence he'd always antici-pated it to be. He'd hidden his reaction that night, but the heat between them had been fierce and elemental—to the point that in the last six months not one woman had made it into his bed. The memory of his future wife and the reality of her rapidly approaching twenty-first birthday had rendered him all but impotent.

With irritation mounting at this acknowledgement of the

power she seemed to hold over him so effortlessly, Rafael studied the photograph on the desk before him. It was of Isobel, running across a busy street in Paris, arm in arm with a handsome young man. Even though Rafael knew already that the man in question was her dance partner, and gay, it didn't stop the surge of hot anger in his belly. It was as if Isobel was mocking him.

To compound this feeling, Isobel was smiling broadly, with clearly not a care in the world, eyes sparkling with humour and *beauty*. Rafael's gut tightened. He'd been right, but even he had underestimated the full force of Isobel's beauty. The hint of teenage puppy fat had disappeared, to reveal the exquisite bone structure of her face. She'd had her hair cut short—very short—and while Rafael didn't ordinarily find short hair attractive, on Isobel it highlighted those huge eyes and the delicate lines of her jaw and neck, making her look both incredibly seductive and innocent.

Something that felt absurdly like regret rushed through Rafael as he acknowledged that there could be no way Isobel was still the blushing virgin he'd encountered on the night of her eighteenth birthday. It would be impossible. But he didn't know why regret was surfacing, when he'd never had any desire to bed a virgin and had more or less *instructed* Isobel to become a woman.

Rafael's mouth firmed. Well, she'd done that, and then some. She'd left Buenos Aires within weeks of their meeting and gone to Paris, where she'd been making a living teaching Argentine Tango dance classes. She hadn't used her extensive and expensive British education to carve out a high-profile career or social existence, and as a result had gone unnoticed as far as the tabloids were concerned. As time had passed Rafael had had to admit to a growing sense of respect. The periodic reports that he received showed that she was living in the most basic of accommodation, and struggling to survive just like anyone else.

He knew she was receiving no hand-outs from her parents because they had nothing to give. Their finances were in a sorry state after years of bad judgments and investments. They had come to him some weeks before, and he had assured them that he fully intended to go through with the marriage and instructed them to leave all the arrangements up to him. Their relief had been palpable.

Rafael turned around in his chair and looked out of the window at the view of Plaza de Mayo, the business hub of Buenos Aires. He rested his chin on steepled fingers. Within minutes of meeting Isobel that night she'd effectively blasted apart any misconception he'd had about her character. Clearly she was not cut of the same cloth as other girls in her peer group, and her actions since then had only confirmed that.

A sense of anticipation coiled in his belly. The time had come to bring his fiancée home and get married. She looked far too carefree and happy in the photograph he'd just received. And the memory of that kiss was too tantalisingly erotic.

Exactly as his solicitor had warned, and as he knew himself, his business was starting to suffer. Clients and colleagues were growing nervous, thinking that his single status translated to his being less than reliable on all fronts. He was more often than not in social situations the only single man. He never thought he'd say it, but he could now see the advantages that his marriage had to offer—not the least of which was the prospect of a stunningly beautiful wife on his arm and in his bed.

This was a business decision, pure and simple, and would be a marriage of convenience like a thousand others in his city.

* * *

'That's right, Lucille, keep bringing your feet back together. Marc, watch your embrace. It needs to be much firmer—you're not giving Lucille enough support...'

Isobel adjusted the couple who had just danced past her and watched as they set off again, her eyes automatically going to the other dancers in her tango class, assessing their progress.

Unfortunately, they couldn't distract her from the humiliating fact that since she'd left Buenos Aires, a few weeks after the fateful night of her eighteenth birthday, she hadn't managed to get through one day without thinking about Don Rafael Ortega Romero. Or seeing his devastating face and body in her mind's eye.

She'd done everything she could to try and block out his words and what had passed between them. *That kiss.* Even now she got hot just thinking about it. And, despite living in one of the most cosmopolitan cities in the world, with men asking her out regularly, she'd yet to come close to experiencing anything like she had with Rafael that night.

If she went on a date, at some point she'd begin to compare her date's lovemaking to Rafael's kiss, or how it had felt to be in his arms, and a coldness would lodge in her chest and make her push him back. It was as if Rafael had put some kind of spell on her that night, and she hated him for it.

The back of her neck prickled then, as if thinking about him might conjure him up, and she shook off the feeling with an effort that dismayed her. This year, for the first time, she'd stopped jumping at every sudden movement, or when someone tapped her on the shoulder. From the moment she'd got off the plane in Paris she'd been expecting to see Rafael. Expecting him to haul her back to Buenos Aires, incensed that she had run away.

Isobel shook her head now, disgusted with herself all over

again. *Why* hadn't she been able to erase the memory of that kiss three years ago? She was disgusted too because never in a million years had she ever wanted to be in thrall to someone like him. Arrogant and rich, taking everything for granted.

A small voice pointed out that her judgment of him was purely superficial, but Isobel disregarded it. She knew very well the kind of world he came from, because she came from it, too. And nothing could dissuade her from believing that he would be as amoral and greedy as the next billionaire, whose sole focus was keeping up appearances and making money. It had been there in his arrogant stance that night of her eighteenth birthday, when he'd come to look her over like a brood mare he was considering buying.

As time had worn on she'd almost started to believe that perhaps she'd dreamt it—perhaps Rafael hadn't really meant it when he'd insisted that they would be married. But just weeks ago she'd felt a cold finger of fear touch her spine when her mother had been far too genial on the phone during one of their sporadic calls.

Her parents had fought her decision to go to Paris, but Isobel had insisted, and since then relations had been strained. When Isobel's mother had sounded so uncharacteristically upbeat, Isobel had had a strong suspicion that they knew something she didn't. Had Rafael been in touch with them? Had he reassured them that he and Isobel would be married? She couldn't ignore the fact that it was two weeks from her twenty-first birthday. Her belly clenched into a knot of tension.

The song playing through the speakers came to an end and Isobel welcomed the distraction. She clapped her hands together and faced her students, lamenting again the fact that her regular partner, José, was ill and couldn't be there to teach with her.

'We're almost done, but I'll show you how we can put

all these steps together in a sequence. Now, I just need a volunteer...'

Isobel looked around the group and groaned inwardly. None of the men was really good enough to do a demo. But just as she was about to select the best of the bunch, she noticed that everyone's attention had gone over her head to something behind her, where the door to the studio was. The tiny hairs stood up on the back of her neck again, and with a nearly overwhelming sense of foreboding she turned around.

Rafael had to curb the violence of the reaction in his body when Isobel turned to face him. It was like nothing he'd ever experienced in his life. Even though he'd had regular updates on her activities, and photographs, it hadn't prepared him to see her in the flesh, up close, with her light scent suffusing the air.

She was dressed in black knee-length leggings and a tank top, showing off the slender gracefulness of her dancer's physique. She wore special dance shoes, which were obviously more practical for teaching a class than the requisite high heels, but already Rafael was imagining her feet encased in silver or gold, slim high heels elongating those gorgeous legs.

Just as he'd seen in the photograph, her short hair made her delicate features stand out, made her more luminously beautiful. Her eyes were the same: huge pools of dark brown velvet, their lashes long and dark. She was exquisite. His blood got hot, and as he watched every ounce of colour drained from her face completely.

Isobel felt the urge to reach out and hold on to something concrete. Don Rafael Ortega Romero stood just feet away from her, dwarfing her tiny studio. For an awful second she wondered if she was in fact imagining him standing there, if she was experiencing some kind of hallucination brought on by thinking about him… But then he spoke.

'I think I could be of assistance to you, if you need a dance partner…?'

Isobel felt paralysed. She couldn't react, couldn't speak. She was dimly aware of her students looking curiously from her to Rafael.

'To demonstrate the steps?' Rafael prompted, as if she might be having trouble understanding him. As if it was entirely normal that he'd just turned up in her place of work, on the other side of the world.

Isobel saw Rafael take off his dark jacket, revealing a white shirt and dark trousers. She felt a ripple of unmistakable feminine interest spike behind her and it seemed to break her out of the shock threatening to suck her under.

Taking control, she put out a hand. 'No, it's fine—really, I'll use…' She looked around and thought wildly for a second, but this was the beginners' class. Her eyes rested on Marc, but he went red and gave her a tortured look. Her heart sank. She couldn't do it to him. She looked back at Rafael, who was standing there looking smug with arms crossed.

'Do you know how to dance tango?' Isobel asked, feeling as if she'd been dropped into some surreal world. She didn't even think she was breathing.

Rafael smiled arrogantly. 'I'm Argentinian—of course I know how to tango. I've been dancing since my grandmother used to sneak my brother and I into *milongas* when we were younger.'

Isobel was stunned into speechlessness, and only the presence of curious eyes forced her to pretend insouciance, to shrug lightly and turn round to start the music. With shaking fingers she chose a song, and the strains of Carlos Di Sarli wound through the studio. Numb with shock, she turned back to face Rafael, who was now standing in front of her with a quirked brow.

'What are we doing?'

'*Ochos* and *sacadas*.'

He nodded. Isobel couldn't delay any longer, or the song would be over and her students would be wondering who this enigmatic stranger was and why she was acting so weirdly. She walked forward and into his arms. He took her hand and settled an arm across her back, and Isobel closed her eyes in a moment of desperation; his touch was having an explosive effect on her insides.

On the balls of her feet, she moved so that she leant into him fully, and then expertly Rafael started to dance, twisting and turning Isobel in a series of moves to demonstrate the steps she'd mentioned.

Isobel dimly recognised in some rational part of her brain that he danced like a professional. Her natural dance ability and instinct took over as she recognised his lead and followed him. She unconsciously let him take more of her weight. The steps became more complex. For the first time in her life, despite dancing with many partners, tango suddenly felt *sexy*, and she wished he wasn't holding her so close. Her head was turned in the same direction as his, tucked perfectly just below his jaw. They *fitted* perfectly.

She was aware of Rafael's steel band of support across her back, her right hand held high by his. She was aware of his arm under her shoulder, her hand spread across his back. She could feel the muscles bunch and move as he danced, and only the fact that she was such an experienced dancer stopped her from tripping over her own feet.

It was a long moment before Isobel realised that the music had stopped and they weren't dancing any more. With a jerky move she pulled herself free of Rafael's arms and stood apart, none too steady. She felt hot in the face. Her students were looking at her with slightly open-mouthed expressions that Isobel couldn't and didn't want to decipher.

She got caught up in a flurry of goodbyes and thank yous, was touched when some of her students presented her with small gifts, but through it all she felt as if she were on a tight-rope of tension, acutely aware of the man who lounged non-chalantly just feet away, waiting for her.

Was it time? Had he come to bring her home? She was very much afraid she was about to find out.

Isobel walked back into the studio after changing in the tiny bathroom next door. Her heart kicked to see that Rafael was still there. He hadn't been some bizarre hallucination. She felt self-conscious and shabby in an ancient knee-length sundress. It had been unbearably hot even by early morning that day, and she'd thrown on the coolest thing that came to hand. Next to the stunning perfection of Rafael she felt like a bag lady.

Her pulse sped up when she saw Rafael turn from where he'd been looking out of the window over the street below. His hands were in his pockets and his eyes looked her up and down, their expression shuttered.

He gestured towards where a couple of gift-wrapped boxes sat by her things. 'Do your students know that it's your birthday in two weeks?'

Isobel looked at Rafael, panic resounding through her in waves. *He'd come for her.*

'It's nearly three years to the day since we met, Isobel, do you remember?'

Her mouth felt numb. She'd gone icy cold. She deliberately ignored what he said. 'They're not birthday gifts. I'm shutting down for August as everyone in Paris goes on their holidays. Some students bring me small gifts to say thank you.'

Rafael just looked at her with that intent gaze. In a bid to put some space between them and turn her back to him, Isobel went over to her things and started to pack up her iPod and speakers, putting it all into a small backpack. Her brain had seized.

When everything was packed away she turned around and took a deep breath, steeling herself. Her belly went into a tight knot of apprehension. 'Why are you here, Mr Romero?'

His dark eyes speared her to the spot. 'You know very well why I'm here. And it's not Mr Romero. It's *Rafael*.'

Isobel's hand clenched on her bag. Even now, when he'd confirmed why he'd come, she tried to deny it to herself—fool herself into thinking that she still had some sort of choice. 'I'm not prepared to just—'

He cut her off. 'We're not going to discuss this here and now. I'll have my car pick you up from your apartment at 7:00 p.m. and bring you to my hotel.'

Isobel nearly fainted to think that he was just snapping his fingers and expecting her to fall in behind him. Hysteria wasn't far from her voice. 'How do you know I don't have plans? That I don't have friends I've arranged to meet somewhere? If you think you can just come here and pluck me out of my life like this—'

Rafael stepped close, and Isobel fought strenuously not to move back a pace. His eyes roved over her face, making her skin prickle.

'You've known very well this day was coming, and you can't say I haven't left you alone to enjoy your independence. I've booked a table for dinner this evening and you *will* join me.'

While Isobel was still absorbing her shock at his implacable arrogance, he'd somehow taken her bag off her shoulder and with a hand on her elbow was escorting her from the studio. He'd taken her keys and was locking up behind them, as if he did it all the time.

Once they stepped out into the street, the languorous city heat did little to break Isobel from her inertia. Rafael calmly handed her back her keys and bag and indicated a sleek car parked by the kerb. 'I won't offer you a lift, as I know you live just a block away from here, but my car will be waiting for you at seven.'

He reached out and trailed a finger down Isobel's cheek to her jaw. It left a line of fire in its wake, making her breath hitch, shocking her out of the inertia holding her in its grip. He'd done exactly the same thing that night three years before.

'Don't try anything silly, Isobel, or I'll just come for you myself.'

And then, speechless, Isobel just watched as Don Rafael Ortega Romero got into the back of the car and it pulled away and disappeared into the traffic.

Isobel was still in a state of shock three hours later. She looked at her reflection in the cracked mirror that lay against a wall in the tiny space the landlord euphemistically called a bedroom. She'd found the mirror one day in a nearby skip and carried it home.

She knew well the kind of man Rafael was. The world he came from was a place where people didn't say no to him, so she knew his threat was not an empty one. He wouldn't stand for being stood up. A disturbing frisson of something she didn't want to name went through her belly and she quashed it. She hated the fact that she seemed to be caught up in wondering about what Rafael thought of her now.

In a moment of weakness about a year ago she'd done a

Google search on him, to see where he was, what he was doing, and she'd seen a picture of him at a premiere in Los Angeles with a veritable glamazon of a woman on his arm. All long, luscious limbs and flowing red hair. The kind of woman Isobel didn't think she could *ever* hope to imitate.

She looked at her hair critically; she'd had it cut when she'd come to Paris on an impulse. It had felt like something rebellious, something cathartic, to distract her from the fact that she couldn't escape her fate. Sometimes now, though, she longed for length again—something to hide behind. She'd felt acutely exposed today under Rafael's gaze.

She gave herself a last, dismissive look, collected her bag and went down to wait for the car. It was only in the car on the way to Rafael's hotel that Isobel realised that not once since she'd seen Rafael again that afternoon had the thought occurred to her to try and run or escape.

Rafael sat in the lobby of the Plaza Athénée hotel and waited for Isobel. It was one of the grandest hotels in Paris, but Rafael didn't notice the trappings of wealth around him, the expensive scents of the women there as they passed by with unconcealed looks of interest in his direction.

A coil of delicious tension snaked through his body—a sense of anticipation he hadn't felt in a long, long time. He remembered the moment in that study three years before, when Isobel had stood up to him, taking him by surprise, and he recognised the same sense of anticipation.

He saw his car pull up outside the main door and stood, grimacing slightly when he felt that tight coil of tension move southwards. With ruthless control he called his body to heel. And then the minute he saw Isobel's silhouette emerge from the car that control was blasted to smithereens.

She passed two men as she walked in the main entrance, and Rafael saw how they both turned to look. He was no better, with his eyes glued to the graceful curve of her body. She wore the unmistakable signs of her breeding unconsciously; her dress was most likely chainstore, and nothing more than plain and black…but it could have been a Dior creation the way it hugged her torso and clung softly to her slim thighs, flaring out slightly at the knee. His eyes dropped to see her feet encased in silver high-heeled sandals and his desire escalated. With a burst of pique at his uncontrollable hormones, he went to intercept her.

Isobel tried not to be intimidated by the plush luxury of the iconic Paris hotel. It was a long time since she'd been somewhere so opulent, and she found it a little overpowering now. If she'd felt like a bag lady earlier, now she felt as if she might be mistaken for a cleaner.

She went towards the reception desk, with the intention of getting them to inform Rafael that she was here. She was not expecting the great man to be waiting himself. But just then something tall and dark caught her eye. She turned to see Rafael, in a coal-black suit and white shirt, striding across the marble lobby towards her. Isobel quailed inwardly. He looked angry, a glower transforming his features as he came closer and closer. She felt a hot rush of sensation when she remembered the tango they'd danced earlier and how closely he'd held her.

He came to a stop just inches away, and Isobel was more nervous than she cared to admit, reacting testily to his obvious irritation. 'There's no need to look like you're about to take my head off. I'm only too happy to turn around and go home.'

For a second she saw Rafael battle with something, and then the glower was gone, replaced by a smile so gorgeous and charming that she was sorry she'd said anything. He put a disturbingly warm hand on her elbow.

'Come through to the bar. We'll have an aperitif before dinner.'

Isobel had no choice but to follow him. His hand was like a steel brand on her elbow, and heat radiated up her arm. No other man had ever had such a viscerally intense physical reaction on her body. To her relief when they walked into the bar he let her go, so they could sit down at a table. The décor was a sophisticated mix of modern and antique, the lighting was low and the tones of conversation around them reverentially hushed. Soft piano music played in the background.

She'd dreaded this moment of seeing Rafael again for three years, and yet now that it was here it didn't feel as if it was dread making her belly tighten...

A bowing waiter materialised, as if from thin air, and Rafael looked at Isobel. She felt flustered and hot. 'I'll...just have a sparkling water, please.'

Rafael just looked at her, before glancing at the waiter and saying, 'A shot of whisky. No ice. Thank you.'

The waiter walked away and Rafael settled back into his chair, long legs stretched out under the table. Isobel's usual sense of co-ordination and grace had deserted her somewhere back in the lobby. She felt as tightly wound as a spring and sat straight, legs tucked under her chair, as far away from his as she could get.

The corner of his mouth tipped up in a small smile and her chest literally ached for a second.

'I have to admit it, Isobel, you've surprised me and proved me wrong.'

She schooled her body and mind's traitorous responses

and replied tightly, 'I wasn't aware that I was doing anything with *you* in mind.'

His smile grew. 'You threw down the gauntlet when you left Buenos Aires.'

'I also told you that I never wanted to see you again.'

He smiled. 'Well, you knew that wasn't going to happen.'

Isobel felt the colour leaching from her face like a physical reaction, draining all the way down to her feet. *No escape.*

He continued. 'I've kept tabs on you, and believe me, if I'd thought it necessary I would have come for you a lot sooner.' He shrugged minutely and almost smirked. 'But it would appear that your closest association has been with your gay dance partner, so I wasn't too worried.'

Heat flooded Isobel's cheeks at his *'I would have come for you a lot sooner.'* 'You had me followed?'

Rafael shrugged again, and grimaced delicately. 'I wouldn't say *followed*, per se, I merely had access to your movements. After all, you are essentially my fiancée.'

Fury raced through Isobel, and she seized the opportunity to feel righteous, with something concrete to be angry about. 'You had me followed, and that is unacceptable.'

She stood up, but in an instant Rafael was standing, too, dwarfing her across the table. His face wasn't remotely charming now.

'Sit down, Isobel. I will not allow you to use something so flimsy as an excuse to walk out of here just because I make you feel nervous.'

Shock upon shock reverberated through her. Isobel's jaw felt sore from clenching it. She felt as transparent as a glass screen, but lied, 'You don't make me nervous. And I'm not going to stay unless you apologise for having me followed.'

Tension crackled between them. Rafael's eyes glowed, a

dark and almost black-brown, and Isobel had a sudden flash of memory, back to when he'd kissed her and she'd seen flecks of green in their depths. She felt weak.

Rafael struggled not to kick the low table out of the way and haul her into his arms, crush her mutinous mouth under his. Two spots of colour were in her cheeks, standing out against the pallor that lingered, evidence of her discomfiture.

Easily, because it cost him nothing, he said, 'I apologise. Now sit down.' When she didn't move straight away he bit out, 'Please.'

Finally she sat, and an enticing scent teased his nostrils—*her* scent. Rafael sat, too, and shifted in his seat so he could be comfortable—which was a challenge when his body seemed determined to respond to rogue hormones and not logic. Sexual frustration was not a state he'd ever known until the last six months, and right now it was screaming through his veins.

The waiter came back and put down their drinks. Isobel reached for her water and lifted it to take a big gulp, but just before she did she saw Rafael's glass lifted, too, towards her. He raised a brow.

She blushed, embarrassed, and clinked her glass to his faintly.

'To your health.'

She mumbled something incoherent, her eyes glued to his as they both took a sip. The sparkling fizzy water burst down her throat and brought her back to some sort of reality.

'So tell me,' he drawled, 'how has it been for you living in Paris?'

Isobel looked at him, and he could see her bite her lower lip. He wanted to reach across and take her chin between his fingers, kiss that spot. She looked down and up again, something fleeting crossing her face, before she asked in a strangled voice, 'You want to talk about my life here in Paris?'

Rafael sat forward, elbows on his knees, intent on this woman in a way he hadn't felt about any woman in a very long time. 'That's exactly what I want.'

Isobel sneaked a glance at Rafael. Tension had been gradually building in her body since they'd moved into the plush and opulent dining room, lit with a thousand glinting lights from intricately heavy chandeliers. A waiter came and unobtrusively cleared their empty plates. If asked, she knew she wouldn't remember what they'd eaten, delicious though it had been. Rafael lifted the white wine bottle and gestured to Isobel. She'd only had a few sips from her glass. She shook her head quickly.

Rafael refilled his own glass and shot her a look. 'You don't drink?'

Isobel grimaced slightly. 'I don't have the head for it.' Desperation mounted inside her as she watched him take a lazy sip. She couldn't believe that there was no way out of the situation, and in that moment something else struck her—a feeling of guilt at knowing that he had once tried to forge his own path, marry for love, and it had been destroyed, all because of this legal agreement.

Isobel leant forward. 'Mr Romero…' she faltered. 'That is, Rafael…you can't want to marry me. Neither one of us wants this. Is there no other way we can salvage the agreement without marrying?'

Rafael leant forward, too, putting down his glass. His face was hard, his voice arctic. 'No, Isobel, there is no other way. And you're quite wrong. I *do* want this marriage. The sooner you come to terms with the fact that we are getting married, the better. If we were to try and get out of this agreement the legalities would tie up any monies from the estate for the foreseeable future—a situation your parents really cannot afford. And, as I've told you before, I'm not about to jeopardise one of my most valuable assets.'

CHAPTER THREE

RAFAEL continued, with no clue as to the meltdown going on inside Isobel's head. 'I almost lost a lucrative deal just a month ago, because my client didn't believe I was a secure bet.' He grimaced. 'He was a family man, and viewed my single status as an indication of a lack of stability which he somehow linked to my business practice. It was only when I explained to him that I was engaged to be married that he came back on board.'

Isobel sat back. If Rafael had told one person, the whole of Buenos Aires would now know. No wonder her mother had sounded so complacent. Rafael kept talking, watching her carefully, his dark eyes focused on her, and Isobel felt as though she'd been hit by a lorry.

'So you see, Isobel, the wheels have been set in motion. The press has already been speculating about my upcoming nuptials.'

Isobel's mouth opened, even though she hadn't even formulated anything to say, but Rafael lifted a hand. 'Let me finish.'

She shut her mouth. She wasn't capable of doing much else.

'On the day of our wedding your parents will receive the money owing to them for the sale of the *estancia*.'

Isobel blankly looked down and saw her cappuccino. She hadn't even registered the waiter delivering it. Her whole life was reduced to this moment in time. She saw everything in a flash: her strict upbringing, her parents' incessant arguments, the respite of her boarding school in Britain and the influence of her staunchly middle-class English relations.

All her dreams seemed to wither into ashes at her feet. She had never stood a chance of escaping this fate. She looked back up to Rafael and found her voice. It sounded husky. 'I haven't changed my mind. You're still the last man on this earth I would choose to marry.'

He looked completely unperturbed. 'What's the problem, Isobel? You've made your point, and commendably. No one would deny that you meant it when you left Buenos Aires to pursue your independence. You've earned my respect. Clearly you're not a gold-digger or a spoilt brat.'

'Wow.' Isobel's short sharp laugh had a slightly hysterical edge. 'Thanks for the compliment.'

He ignored her. 'But the fact remains you have a duty and a role to fulfil—a life *with* me back in Buenos Aires. You didn't really expect to escape for ever, did you? What was your plan? To live a step above squalor, teaching tango for the rest of your life? Fall in love with a humble dancer, settle down and have babies?'

The derision in his voice finally broke through Isobel's shock. She sat up straight, shaking all over. 'That's *exactly* what I had planned. Right along with a small cottage with a white picket fence, roses around the door and the human right of being free, allowed to live my life the way I want. Just because I was born into a certain society—does not mean that I'm beholden to it.'

Rafael smiled cynically, and his voice held a bitter edge. 'Ah, if only that were true. You and me, Isobel, we *are* constrained by our society, and by our obligation to our backgrounds and our families. You come attached to an estate worth millions. Not even you can walk away from that responsibility without damaging those closest to you.'

Before Isobel could react Rafael had smoothly taken something out from the inside pocket of his jacket. It was a velvet box. Isobel's brain was starting to implode. She watched warily as Rafael handed it across the table to her. She had a sudden pathological fear of touching the box.

Barely stifling his irritation at her less than interested response, Rafael flipped the lid up to reveal a stunning glittering diamond bracelet.

'It's just an early token for your birthday, Isobel...and a taste of what you can expect in the future as my wife.'

Isobel stilled in shock. She put down her napkin. 'I thought we'd established that I'm not a gold-digger.'

'That doesn't mean you can't accept a gift and enjoy it. Take it, Isobel.'

Isobel knew that she'd have to be held down and restrained before she'd accept the bracelet. She stood up shakily. Rafael made a move to stop her, and Isobel looked at him haughtily. 'I presume I'm still free to go to the bathroom?'

Rafael inclined his head and watched her walk away a little unsteadily. He closed the lid of the box and placed it back on the table. He brooded. He hadn't expected her to turn green at the sight of a stunning diamond bracelet, no matter how principled she was. He also hadn't expected her to resist when he came for her. He had to admit he'd expected at least some sense of resignation. She surely hadn't believed that she'd never have to return and take her place, take up her role? Was she completely delusional?

He flicked a glance at his watch. She'd been gone ten minutes. He looked at the doors; no sign of her return. And he knew right then, with a cold rage filling his chest, that she'd run out on him. Coolly, he motioned for the bill. He had a plan for the future and Isobel was it—whether she liked it or not.

'You and me, Isobel, we are *constrained by our society, and by our obligation to our backgrounds…'* The words reverberated in Isobel's head, along with the image of that diamond bracelet. Tears pricked her eyes. She couldn't believe that her life as an independent woman was being so comprehensively threatened. She couldn't go so far as to say to herself that it was over, because that meant defeat and that she had no choice.

At that moment, though, as if to confuse her utterly, Isobel had a memory of her grandmother, just before she'd died, telling her that one day she would inherit the *estancia*. But of course that had been before they'd sold it to Rafael's father. She'd been only six when her grandmother had died.

She could barely remember the *estancia*, as it had been so long since she'd seen it, but she did remember that it had felt like an enchanted place. It was where her grandparents had met, and she'd heard the romantic story many times.

Despite their own arranged marriage, her grandparents had been truly in love. It had pervaded everything around them. Isobel knew now that her grandmother's death had sent her grandfather off the rails, and that was when he had started to gamble and drink too heavily, incurring great losses which had undoubtedly led to his need to sell the *estancia*…and this situation.

She could remember the way her grandfather had looked at her grandmother after they'd danced a tango together, oblivious to everyone around them… Isobel had always vowed that she too would marry for love, and not get sucked into a cold, sterile marriage like so many she'd seen growing up. Going to school in England had given her the false illusion that she was in control of her destiny. But she hadn't been— not since the age of eight, when events outside of her control had taken place.

An uncomfortable voice pointed out to Isobel that in the past three years she *hadn't* met the elusive love of her life, but she quashed it. Don Rafael Ortega Romero was the last man on earth she'd find that connection with. And if he thought for a second that she'd meekly go home just because it was the right thing to do, he had another think coming. She couldn't give up on her dream so easily, no matter what was at stake. There *had* to be another way out.

Despite the way she'd felt hot under his gaze all evening, she couldn't imagine for a second that he actually *fancied* her. She didn't like the way that thought sank right to the depths of her belly like a stone, but at least it meant that perhaps she could appeal to him on that level. Why would he want to shackle himself to a wife he wasn't even attracted to?

Isobel's Métro pulled into her station. She felt mildly guilty for having run out on Rafael, but at the same time she knew that it was only his ego that would be dented.

As she climbed the steps out of the metro and emerged back into the warm air of the dark evening she felt a horribly familiar prickling feeling. So she wasn't all that surprised to see Rafael waiting for her, leaning casually against a wall. Isobel averted her eyes, ignored the betraying kick of her heart, and started to walk purposefully to her apartment, just a couple of blocks away. Rafael kept pace with her easily.

'I didn't think you were brought up to walk out on a dinner date, Isobel.'

Isobel flushed, embarrassed despite her best intentions. 'I wasn't. But for certain people I'll make an exception. Especially when the conversation descends to farce.'

'There's not many women who would consider marriage with me farcical, Isobel. I have to say that you're unique.'

Isobel had to step aside to avoid bumping into an old lady. Immediately, she felt Rafael's arms around her, steadying her. She broke away jerkily. They reached her door and Isobel prayed that her hand wouldn't shake as she unlocked it. This man disturbed her more every time she saw him, threatening her on many more levels than she cared to admit to.

When she'd opened the door he drawled easily, 'Aren't you going to ask me in for a coffee?'

Isobel turned in the doorway and looked up, thankful that his face was somewhat obscured by the dark. 'No, I'm not.'

She started to close the door in his face, but he was too quick and easily stopped it closing. This time a steel thread ran through his voice. 'Well, tough, because I'm coming in. We haven't finished talking.'

He was immovable. Isobel knew with a sinking feeling that he wouldn't budge. Now or ever. She was fighting a losing battle. Silently she stood back.

Isobel took a certain satisfaction in having Rafael endure her tiny and cramped studio apartment. Undoubtedly he was used to far more salubrious surroundings. All she had separating her bedroom area from her sitting room/kitchen was an old clothes rail with a sheet draped over it.

Even so, Rafael's huge and charismatic presence made her want to get him out of there as soon as possible, so she busied herself making coffee, noticing that Rafael had a good look around before sitting down and dwarfing her one decent chair.

She handed him a steaming cup. 'It's instant,' she said sweetly. 'I hope you don't mind.'

'Not at all,' he replied, equally sweetly, and took the cup from her.

Isobel moved away and leant against the counter of the kitchen, crossed her arms over her chest. Rafael took his time sipping the coffee before he put the cup down on a low table in front of him and leant forward, arms on his knees.

He looked at her from under hooded lids with an unmistakably cynical gleam in his eyes. 'Are you telling me that if I'd pretended that we weren't bound by a legal decree to wed, that if I'd alluded to some romantic feelings and couched a proposal in the language of hearts and flowers, you would have accepted, Isobel?'

His words impacted upon her in her solar plexus like a punch to the gut, and they shouldn't. Panic gripped her. Had he seen something of the tender inner core of her? 'Of course not,' she scoffed. 'I know you don't have a heart, or else you wouldn't be agreeing to such a cold union.'

Rafael stood, and Isobel instinctively backed away hurriedly, but realised that the counter was at her back. He was instantly menacing and darkly threatening, and Isobel was reminded that once upon a time he *had* had a heart, had wanted to marry someone he was passionate about. The thought lacerated her now.

He arched a brow and came closer. 'Cold, Isobel? On the contrary, I don't plan on this *union* being cold at all. In fact, right now I feel that it could be very hot.'

Isobel just looked at him speechlessly as he advanced. He was so tall and dark, even more so than she remembered. The memory of that kiss sent a wave of heat through her body. If he suspected for a second— She put out a restraining hand in panic, in case he might find out just how vulnerable she felt inside. 'I didn't mean it like that.' Her brain scrabbled for words. 'I meant… I just meant that—'

Rafael was so close now that Isobel had to look up. One more step and her hand would be pressed against his chest. And then he took that step, and sensation exploded. 'Let's see exactly how cold this marriage will be, hmm?'

Before Isobel could evade him he'd stepped right up to her, so that her hand was pressed right into a hard wall of muscle and his two hands were around her head, caressing her skull. As if time had slowed down his head lowered and lowered, until nothing remained but heat and his mouth settling over hers like a firebrand.

Her other hand clutched the counter behind her. It was the only thing stopping her from falling down as the rush of sensation made her legs weak. Rafael's mouth moved over hers with expert precision, teasing, tasting. But then any teasing was gone as his mouth firmed and became a ruthless pressure, dominating her with sensual ease. Exactly as it had that night three years before, and as no other man had done in the interim.

Isobel didn't have the defences for this onslaught. She was crippled by how awfully familiar his touch now felt. Her lips parted instinctively and Rafael uttered a groan deep in his throat, his hands leaving her head to descend over her body and haul her in closer to his lean length.

When his tongue touched hers Isobel was horrified to hear a mewl coming from her throat, but she couldn't stop herself from responding. Desperately, on some rational level, she tried to… But it was impossible. Her whole body was going up in flames, her back arching to press even closer to Rafael's chest, between her thighs pulsing with desire.

With a shocking move Rafael thrust one hard thigh

between her legs, and Isobel felt an explosion of hot, wet lust at her core. His hand moved up over the curve of her waist and cupped one breast, his thumb moving back and forth over the thin material, making her nipple tighten painfully against the fabric.

He moved his hips and she felt his burgeoning arousal. Isobel tore her mouth away, breathing harshly, to stare up into triumphant and mocking eyes. His hand caressed her breast intimately. Her soul withered to know that he'd so easily exerted his dominance over her, and with all her strength she brought her hands to his chest and pushed hard.

When he finally moved back after a long moment it killed Isobel to know that he'd done so out of his own choice and not through any action on her part. She was like a puny kitten next to him.

On shaky legs Isobel moved to the other side of the room. Her whole body tingled and burned in the aftermath. She turned to face Rafael, feeling utterly undone and unbelievably vulnerable.

'Like I said,' he drawled, apparently unmoved, 'I think the least of our worries will be the fact that this union has no heat. You've matured into a beautiful woman, Isobel—'

Feeling acutely threatened, Isobel lashed out. 'The kind of woman you can take into your bed? Isn't that what you said that night? Well, that's handy for you isn't it?'

Panic tinged her voice. Her one flimsy plan of action—counting on the fact he didn't find her attractive—was being destroyed right before her eyes. Even though she had little experience, it would appear that Rafael *did* find her attractive. Isobel should have found that realisation devastating, and she *did*, but for all the wrong reasons.

Rafael looked unperturbed and still triumphant. 'Very

handy, I'd say. It will be a cornerstone for a strong and successful marriage.'

His eyes dropped down her body, making her heart speed up.

'If you're concerned about my fidelity,' he drawled seductively, 'I don't think I'll have a problem with that.'

Sudden heat flared in her belly, much to her disgust, and Isobel bit back a retort. She said through gritted teeth, 'For the umpteenth time, I don't want to marry you, so you shouldn't have to face the boring prospect of *fidelity*.'

Rafael looked serious then, all facetiousness set aside. 'At the risk of repeating myself, and pointing out the inevitable *again*, we have no choice. This marriage *will* take place. It is the only way to ensure that your parents receive what's due to them. And you're forgetting that on our marriage day you will become joint owner of an extremely lucrative estate. One of the biggest in Argentina.'

Isobel flushed at being reminded of their unbreakable ties. And also at being reminded of that nebulous pull she felt to the *estancia* that had been her grandmother's.

Even so, she fought. It was all she had left to do. Her response to him made her lash out again. 'Damn you, Rafael, you think you know it all. It goes against everything in me to bind myself into a loveless marriage to fulfil the terms of some agreement. There has to be another way.'

He smiled a hard smile. 'I'm not a tyrant, Isobel. I won't be locking you away in a high tower.'

Isobel still fought. 'I'd rather be locked in a tower than be forced into an arranged marriage with a cynical, spoilt, jaded Buenos Aires playboy who has nothing better to do than make arrogant demands because he's decided he's happy to honour some ancient agreement.' Isobel realised she was breathing hard. 'I want you to leave.'

An incredulous expression stole across Rafael's face. 'You have no idea, do you?'

Despite herself Isobel had to ask. 'No idea about what?'

Rafael was watching her carefully. 'About how badly your father is doing… He's made some highly risky investments lately, spurred on by your mother, and they've all backfired. He's on the verge of bankruptcy.'

'Oh, please,' Isobel said disgustedly. 'If this is just your attempt to make me feel even more vulnerable—'

'It's not.'

He sounded so grim that Isobel just looked at him, and felt a cold finger of dread touch her spine.

'Your father is in serious trouble, Isobel. He stands to lose everything.'

Isobel instinctively reached for the high-backed chair near her, needing to hold on to something. Right then she knew implicitly that Rafael wouldn't be lying about this. He wouldn't need to. Her father had always had a rash side; it was what had made him a financial whiz in the first place, and brought him to the attention of her mother's family, who'd wanted her to marry into the prestigious and more stable banking world in Europe. Isobel had always suspected that the sale of the *estancia* had probably had as much to do with her father's reckless trading as her grandfather's own poor judgment. And she could well imagine now that the collapse of the global economy hadn't been kind to him.

She tried not to reveal how shaken she was by this news, and recalled that she hadn't heard from her father in some weeks. He'd always made an effort to keep in touch.

'How do you know this?'

Rafael grimaced. 'It seems you've forgotten how small our world is in Buenos Aires. It's not common knowledge yet how bad things are for him, but I'm in close contact with some of his lenders and it's not good. I'd say he has at the most a month before it becomes public knowledge.'

Isobel had gone inward, and she said now, more to herself than Rafael, 'My mother mustn't know…if she knew about this…'

'Oh, she knows all right. That's why they came to see me some weeks ago. Their very future hinges on this marriage going ahead, so needless to say they were extremely relieved when I told them I had it in hand.'

Isobel looked at Rafael. She was stunned. Everything had just been tipped on its axis, and suddenly her last remaining hope of any possible way out was being ripped from under her feet.

As if to ram it home, Rafael spelt it out. 'When we marry, the *estancia* will become half yours, as my wife. Your parents will receive their sizeable inheritance and your family will be fine. And there's something else you should know—the agreement says that I only have to pay half of what the *estancia was* worth, but I've agreed to pay your parents half of what it's worth *now*. Needless to say, we're talking a difference that runs into millions. But I'm prepared to do this as I have no wish for my wife's family to struggle financially in the future.'

And then he stuck the knife in even deeper. 'How can you turn your back on your family when they need you? Or turn your back on receiving the legacy of your grandmother's ancestral home for your own children?'

Isobel had let go of the counter and her fingernails were scoring half-moons in the palms of her hands. She hated Rafael for the sense of responsibility that washed over her in a sickening wave.

Isobel realised she was shaking like a leaf. 'Get out of my

apartment, Mr Romero. You've said what you came to say, now *get out*.'

'Isobel, you know you don't have a choice.'

'Of course I do,' she said desperately, refusing to give up even now. 'There's always a choice. And I'm not going to ask you again to get out.'

She walked over to the door and opened it wide. To her intense relief Rafael moved towards it. But he stopped just at the threshold. Isobel tried desperately to ignore the way her skin felt hot and seemed to be stretched tight. She avoided Rafael's eyes.

'I'll come for you tomorrow afternoon, Isobel. It's time to come home and fulfil your duty—to me and your family. Your fate was written a long time ago, and it's bound up with mine—irrevocably.'

'Get out,' Isobel said, almost pleading.

Finally he'd gone, and she heard his steps descending the stairs. Closing the door, she sagged back against it and then her legs gave way. She slithered to the ground and sat like that for a long time, her brain blissfully frozen in a state of shock.

Across Paris Rafael stood at the window of his dimly lit bedroom suite. The Eiffel Tower shone and glistened like a giant bauble outside. He had to admit that he admired Isobel more and more after meeting her again. She was still fighting. A dart of panic gripped his gut for a second. He couldn't be sure that she wouldn't have run again by tomorrow.

He knew, though, that the news of her father's dire straits would have made her stop to think. Rafael frowned. He'd truly never been in this situation before, where a woman patently wanted nothing to do with him. His ego wasn't dented…he knew Isobel *wanted* him. And after that kiss the depth of his own attraction for her had stunned him slightly. It had been near impossible to pull back and not give in to the urge to keep going—to caress her slender curves, pull up her dress to inch his hand up those quivering thighs.

He frowned. If he wasn't mistaken, he'd even hazard a guess that she was still innocent. It was in every skittish move she made when he was near, in the way she'd look at him when she thought he wasn't watching. The way that telling colour stole into her cheeks whenever he got too close. While he couldn't be certain she hadn't had a lover, there had clearly been no one significant.

The thought that she might be a virgin sent a frisson of pure masculine thrill through him and it surprised him. He'd never entertained any kind of romantic notion of bedding a virgin bride. He'd always made sure to gravitate towards women who were experienced and knew how to pleasure him.

One thing was sure: he hadn't lied when he'd promised he would be faithful. He had to concede that the memory of her had hovered over the shoulder of every other woman he'd been with since that night. He hadn't met anyone who had touched some primal part of him as effortlessly as she had. The kiss tonight had just proved that they had explosive chemistry.

He placed a hand on the glass and realised his heart was thumping hard. He was becoming aroused by little more than thinking of Isobel—not a usual effect of any woman who occupied his mind, no matter how seductive.

He *would* have Isobel in his life, and in his bed, as his wife. And once she saw what he could provide for her she'd soon realise how futile it would be to fight him, or her fate. He smiled then. This marriage was beginning to look appealing on many more levels than he might ever have anticipated.

* * *

The following day the weather seemed to be in sympathy with Isobel's mood. Bleak and stormy. She was hollow eyed after a long, sleepless night. Her landlord had just been, and her ears were still ringing from his long rant because she was leaving with no notice. She'd had to fork over some precious cash to appease him, and she'd thought a little hysterically of the fact that within a short space of time she'd be the joint owner of a multi-million-dollar estate.

In the lonely hours in the middle of the night she'd resigned herself to the fact that she had submit to this marriage. All avenues of escape were cut off. Curiously, as soon as she'd articulated the thought, a sense of calm had washed over her— not panic, as she'd expected. It was almost as if the fates were conspiring against her to say, *You were never going to escape this*.

She'd called her dance partner José that morning, and without getting into the whole explanation had just said that she had to leave to go home indefinitely because of a family crisis. He'd been sad, but delighted to think he could take over her classes. It drove home to Isobel how tenuous her links to Paris really were, and that was disturbing. Why hadn't she forged deeper links?

Isobel knew a big part of her was still in shock, not really contemplating the reality that faced her.

A peremptory knock sounded on the door. With her stomach in freefall she took a last glance around what had been her home for the best part of three years and went to the door.

'You don't have much baggage.'

Still feeling exposed and raw from realising how easy it had been to walk away from three years of a life, Isobel was trying her best to block out the far too dominant male all but sprawled across the back seat of the luxury car as they were driven to the airport.

She gritted her teeth and recalled his look of pure disbelief when she'd presented herself at the door of her apartment with one wheelie suitcase.

'Not all of us need possessions and money and real estate to feel validated.'

He chuckled softly, but the sound was anything but friendly. 'Very noble. Are you afraid I'll corrupt you with my debauched and materialistic ways?'

Isobel just clamped her mouth shut and said nothing, watching as Paris gave way outside the car to the start of the gritty suburbs and then the anonymous motorway. She felt all at once clammy and sweaty, and her heart beat a restless tattoo in her chest which got worse every time Rafael made the minutest move. She hated to be so aware of him, and told herself it was only antipathy, not attraction.

He was on the phone now, speaking rapidly in Spanish to someone. Isobel could only make out the gist of the conversation as he was talking about something she had no knowledge of: stocks and shares and bonds. But she was supremely aware of the hand nearest her, gesticulating the emphasis of his words, fingers long and graceful.

He terminated the conversation just as they approached the airport and said, 'We're going straight to the plane. Customs will check your passport and documents there.'

Before Isobel could draw breath, they'd been cleared to go, and she was stepping into a private jet straight out of a magazine spread. The carpet alone felt like stepping onto a cloud. She'd never seen anything so decadently opulent in her life.

'I suppose you're happy with a carbon footprint the size of Everest?'

Rafael had been moving around behind her and stopped. His hands were on his hips when Isobel turned to face him, drawing attention to how lean they were in faded jeans. It was the first time she'd looked directly at him all morning. He was just too beautiful. And the feelings jumping around her belly were far too ambiguous.

'I share this jet with a group of businessmen, one of whom happens to be my older half-brother. Much as I'd like to take a scheduled flight, sometimes it's just not practical—not when I have back-to-back meetings lined up as soon as we return to Buenos Aires. I'm just lucky that my brother happened to be here in Paris at the moment.'

She couldn't even feel mildly chastised at being put in her place. Intense relief that he was going to be busy nearly made Isobel sag back into the seat behind her. She tried to school her expression, but obviously failed.

'No need to look so pleased, Isobel. You'll need some time at home with your family to prepare for the wedding anyway.'

This time she did sag back into the seat, and she asked shakily, hating having to speak the words out loud, as if that was making it more concrete, 'We're getting married on my birthday?'

Rafael came and sat down in the seat on the other side of the aisle, taking out papers from a briefcase and a super slim platinum laptop. 'Yes. Exactly according to the terms laid out in the agreement.'

She looked away with effort, and her hands shook as she did up her seat belt. 'I can't believe you're making me do this.'

In a flash Rafael had surged out of his seat and was leaning over her, hands on the armrests either side of her body. Isobel shrank back into her seat, her heart nearly jumping out of her chest.

'*I'm* not making you do anything Isobel. We're bound

together by a set of circumstances outside of our control.' His mouth became a bitter line. 'This marriage has been set in stone for years and it will happen, whether you like it or not. No fairytale endings here, Isobel.'

Panic at his proximity made her blurt out, 'If I had a choice I wouldn't marry someone like you in a million years.'

His eyes flicked up and down, and Isobel felt her skin grow hot. 'So you keep saying. I'm going to think you're protesting just a little too much if you keep this up.'

Rafael just looked at her for an intensely long moment, and then went back to sit down. With a few feet separating them again Isobel felt her heart slow down and her brain cleared. Was he suggesting that on some level she *wanted* this? That she would *choose* this if given a choice? Nausea rose. She couldn't want this on any level. It went against everything she believed in and wanted for herself.

Isobel stayed silent as they taxied and then took off into the air. She watched as Paris fell away below them, gradually becoming smaller and smaller until it got obscured with clouds and disappeared completely. To her surprise, her dominant feeling as they left wasn't of sadness or even anger, it was a kind of ambivalence. Had it really touched her so superficially?

Far too disturbed to investigate that line of thinking, Isobel got her book out of her bag and pretended to be engrossed. But all the while she was acutely aware of every movement Rafael made just feet away.

CHAPTER FOUR

THEY arrived in Buenos Aires on a cool August morning, with dawn breaking over the horizon, sending crimson ribbons across the sky. For some reason it felt like an omen to Isobel, and she wasn't sure if it was good or bad. She could sense Rafael behind her, urging her on to go down the steps. She had to move forward. She took a deep breath and stepped out. When she came to the bottom of the steps and stood on Argentinian soil for the first time in three years she felt something intangible move within her and thought of her grandparents. To her utter disgust, emotional tears prickled ominously.

Blinking them back and feeling betrayed by her emotions, telling herself it had to be tiredness, jet-lag…anything but the fact that she'd actually missed Buenos Aires…she felt Rafael take her arm and lead her over to a waiting car.

Once they were in the back Isobel sent him a quick glance, disgusted to see that Rafael looked as if he'd just woken from a deep, restorative sleep—which, she had to remind herself, he had. He'd worked for a bit at the start of the flight, they'd eaten a meal, and then he'd reclined his chair and snored softly for the whole flight. Isobel knew because she'd been tense and wound up the whole time, casting him suspicious looks, hating him for sleeping so easily.

'What happens now?' she asked, trying to ignore his perfection.

He faced her. 'What happens now is that I drop you at your house. I've been invited over this evening for dinner, and I'll bring your engagement ring with me. It belonged to my grandmother.'

'Engagement ring…' Isobel repeated weakly, with visions of an enormously ostentatious ruby-red rock surrounded by diamonds.

Rafael frowned, unaware of the horror rising within Isobel at how fast things were moving. He took one of her hands and inspected it, making little fires of sensation race up Isobel's arm. 'Your fingers are slim. I'll probably have to get the size adjusted, but that shouldn't take long…'

Isobel pulled her hand free and choked back the urge to shout at the driver to turn right around and go back to the plane. They were entering the outskirts of BA, and Isobel found that she was experiencing that same welling of emotion she'd had on leaving the plane. Her hands clenched in her lap. *How* could her emotions be so fickle? When she was coming home to be all but marched up the aisle with a gun to her head?

Before long they turned into a familiar road, her road, and the gates of Isobel's house opened smoothly. As they came up the drive Isobel could see that her parents were standing at the door, flanked by the staff on either side. All up and dressed, as if it wasn't ungodly early.

Isobel felt a sense of resignation…and with a heavy heart she knew that she was doing the right thing. Losing everything would have destroyed her parents. As much as they might not be close, they were still her parents, and she loved them. The realisation made her feel very vulnerable as Rafael came around and opened her door.

The next few minutes were a blur, but a few things stood out: how possessive Rafael's arm felt clasped around her waist and how it made a churning mix of emotions run through her; her father's relieved and grateful expression; her mother's insincere tears of joy at having her prodigal daughter returned.

And then Rafael was gone, his car disappearing back down the drive. Isobel actually felt bereft for a moment, as if some kind of anchor was being taken away—which was crazy. But then she was being hustled into the house and the door was shut firmly behind her. If she closed her eyes for a brief moment it was almost as if the last three years hadn't happened...

The next couple of weeks passed in a whirlwind. Isobel felt like Dorothy in Oz, caught up in a tornado of escalating ferocity. As she stood looking out of her bedroom window something glinted in the reflection, catching her attention, and she looked down at the engagement ring on her finger.

That first night she'd come home Rafael had returned for dinner, as he'd promised, with a small box. In front of her parents he'd presented her with the ring, and to Isobel's surprise it had been nothing like she'd expected. It was small and delicate, a rare pink diamond, almost deep purple in colour, surrounded by white diamonds in a circular art deco setting.

And again to her surprise, it had fitted like a glove, needing no adjustment. Rafael had all but smirked when it had fitted snugly on her finger, and his hand had remained on hers for an uncomfortably long time.

Since then she'd seen him only a handful of times, always surrounded by people, and in the past few days not at all— he'd had to fly to the States on business.

The papers had been full of their marriage, and Isobel pored over the articles with a sick fascination. Her blood had run cold, though, when she'd read about the deal he was currently involved in; he'd gone to America to bail out a failing company whose employees were mainly illegal Argentinian immigrants. They had gone there as skilled workers who hadn't been able to find work at home due to the economic downturn.

The papers were full of speculation that Rafael would be helping deport those immigrants and building up the company again with legitimate US employees. While Isobel couldn't condone immigrants working illegally, she felt sick to her core that Rafael would just send people back to the place they'd struggled so hard to leave.

He'd phoned every day, though, and predictably Isobel's thoughts were scrambled as soon as she heard his voice. *How could she be so affected by someone so amoral and ruthless?*

'I'm looking forward to seeing you walk down the aisle to me, Isobel,' he'd said once.

She'd gripped the phone tight, panic a familiar sensation. 'You mean you're looking forward to seeing your bride of convenience walking down the aisle.'

Before he could say anything Isobel had said, 'You might find yourself begging to divorce me in six months' time, and that's not going to look good for your business, either.'

His voice had turned to steel. 'We won't be divorcing *ever*. There is no room for failure in this.'

'Your *hair*, Isobel,' her mother wailed shrilly on the day of the wedding. 'How *could* you have cut it all off like that?'

Isobel didn't answer, knowing her mother didn't really expect her to. And anyway, she wasn't sure if she could speak as she took in her reflection in the mirror. About three people hovered around her, making last-minute tweaks to the wedding dress. Isobel felt slightly removed from it all, but hyper-aware at the same time.

The dress was exquisitely simple. It had been her grandmother's. At first Isobel had protested, feeling far too much of a fraud because her grandmother had been so in love when she had got married. But of course her mother wouldn't be swayed. After a few adjustments to update it, it was now strapless, and fell in a simple fitted silken sheath to the floor. Tiny diamonds sewn into a lace overlay sparkled and shone when she moved. And on the back of her head was an antique silver comb which held the long veil in place.

Isobel looked at her reflection in the mirror now and saw the colour surge into her cheeks. She was very much afraid that on some deep, secret level Rafael was affecting her in a way that had nothing to do with logic and common sense. How could it when her disgust at his business ethics was having no effect on her physical reaction to him?

She chastised herself for thinking like that. Her reaction was purely to do with the extreme circumstances of their situation, and the fact that Rafael's sheer masculinity resonated with something in her. She'd never thought she'd react to such an alpha male, but that was all it could be.

She could never develop feelings for a man like him—not in a million years. Her main concern in this marriage would be to seek a way out of it as soon as possible.

Thirty minutes later, with that assertion sill ringing in her head, Isobel stood on her father's arm just outside the open doors of the church. *This was it.* But instead of the barrel full of nerves that Isobel had expected, that she'd hoped would give her the impetus to tear off her veil and run, her reactions confounded her again. A weird calm acceptance was her dominant emotion. And then her father was moving, and she had to move, too.

They stepped into the back of the church and people turned to look. People Isobel recognised vaguely but didn't know. *Society.* The 'Wedding March' was playing, and there at the very top of the aisle stood a tall, broad figure in steel-grey, with thick, wavy, black hair.

Why was it that in this moment of all moments she found herself curiously moved by the thought of the ritual ahead?

Her hand unconsciously tightened on her father's arm, and she didn't see him wince slightly. All she could focus on was Rafael's broad back at the top of the church. With every beat of her heart as she drew closer she superstitiously begged him silently not to turn and look. Because that way she could hate him for being so coolly arrogant and vow to make their marriage as uncomfortable as possible for him. She repeated it like a mantra: *don't turn around, don't turn around*.

But since when had her prayers or wishes been answered? When she was halfway down the long aisle Rafael turned— and not just his head. His whole body turned to face her. Isobel nearly stumbled, and her heart threatened to burst out of her chest. Her blood flowed heavy in her veins. And all she could see was *him*, and those dark eyes boring right through her veil…seeking all her answers. Seeking her soul.

And then her father was handing her over to Rafael, who took her hand to lead her up the steps beside him. He lifted the veil up and over her head, looking down into her eyes with an unmistakable glint of triumph and something very hot. In an instant Isobel was thrown back in time to the study that night, and how she'd felt when she'd looked up into Rafael's eyes for the first time.

He lifted her hand and pressed a kiss to it, and Isobel's brain melted in a puddle of heat and sensation and shock heaped on shock. Because right now the last thing she felt like doing was running away.

The ceremony passed in a blur. Somehow Isobel knew she must have said everything required of her, but she couldn't recall. She was aware of the cool band of gold on her finger.

'…you may now kiss the bride.'

Isobel looked up in shock. They were there already? Rafael had moved closer and brought a hand to the back of her neck. His head was descending, and Isobel could do nothing but let her eyelids flutter closed. Her heart had stopped beating. When the touch of his mouth came to hers she couldn't help a violent tremble, and as if sensing her reaction Rafael put his other hand around her waist, pulling her even closer.

Isobel sensed dimly that Rafael had probably intended the kiss to be a socially suitable chaste touching of his lips to hers, but as soon as they made contact it was as if something bigger took control and they couldn't move apart.

His mouth moved over hers hungrily, as if starved of contact, and to Isobel's shame she felt the same. Her mouth clung with wanton eagerness, lips opening to invite him in, tongue seeking and searching.

It was a discreet cough from the priest that finally broke through the wave of heat that was consuming Rafael. Reluctantly he pulled back, and held in a groan when he saw Isobel's upturned face, so lovely, with a bloom of pink in her cheeks, lips soft and pouting and moist. It took a long second for her to open her eyes, and he read the reactions in their dark chocolate depths: shock, confusion and something much more potent—anger. She hated that she'd reacted to him.

Triumph surged through his body. Isobel would make him a good wife. He knew it deep in his bones. She would match him, stand up to him, and he couldn't wait for tonight when he could get her into his bed. But before the conservative Buenos Aires congregation could read the carnal nature of his thoughts, Rafael turned to lead his wife back up the aisle.

Isobel seethed inwardly as she walked slowly on Rafael's arm. But she managed to paste a fake smile on her face, nodding to people she knew were smiling to her face, but already dissecting every minute of the ceremony, and her dress and the prospects of success for this marriage. They would be the topic of coffee mornings all over the capital for days, weeks to come.

She couldn't believe she'd betrayed herself so badly with her reaction to that kiss. She couldn't believe that at the mere touch of his mouth to hers all her iron-clad intentions had dissolved to dust. This was going to be a lot harder than she'd anticipated because she was so vulnerable to his touch.

She couldn't deny any more that what she felt was not just antipathy to Rafael. What she felt was violent attraction mixed with antipathy, and Isobel knew herself well enough to know that if that intimacy was breached she'd be lost. She'd always believed that physical attraction would be conveniently tied into falling in love with someone. She'd never counted on the fact that it could happen independently of her feelings.

She was terrified now that intimacy with Rafael might result in her deluding herself into thinking that she felt something for him. One thing was paramount as of that moment: she needed to protect herself at all costs, and maintain a distance between them until she knew how to cope with these feelings and not betray herself.

When they emerged from the church, all Isobel's thoughts scattered. A barrage of press awaited them, the camera flashes almost blinding her. And a huge cheering crowd had gathered across the road. Instinctively, her hand tightened on Rafael's arm.

He looked down at her and grimaced slightly before saying, 'I should have expected this. Just smile and look happy. They're all here to see you.'

Isobel was beyond shocked at the reception. After a few minutes Rafael led her down the steps of the huge cathedral and to a waiting car, handing her carefully into the back before joining her.

As they pulled away Isobel saw the rest of the wedding guests start to spill out of the church into the heaving crowds. She realised she was shaking like a leaf. Rafael noticed and took one of her hands in his; to Isobel's dismay her shaking started to subside. Her body was a traitor.

'The reception will be at my house. It's not too far from yours in Recoleta.'

Everything seemed to be impacting upon Isobel at once. She said shakily, 'I've never even been to your house. Was your mother at the church? I don't even know what she looks like—what if she hates me?'

As if Rafael could hear the hint of hysteria in her voice, he said placatingly, 'Yes, she was at the church, and she won't hate you. My house isn't much different to yours, and my older half-brother couldn't make the service, but hopes to come to the reception.' His hand tightened on hers, as if he could see something she was unaware of on her face. 'I thought we'd get there ahead of everyone else so you could have a bit of space.'

At that moment Isobel felt very keenly the absence of a girlfriend—someone who could have been her bridesmaid, someone to confide in. But she'd never had close girlfriends. She'd always wanted such different things from the rest of her peers. And so here she was with Rafael, and *he* was the one to anticipate her need for some time on her own.

She said nothing and took her hand back from his. Before long they were driving through the exclusive suburb of Recoleta, pulling up outside impressive gates. Isobel tried to hide her reaction. This house they were approaching was nothing like her family home. It was grand and palatial on a level that made *her* home look like a gatehouse.

The car pulled up in a gravel courtyard surrounded with flowering trees which kept it secluded and private. An impressive array of vintage cars was lined up on one side, and despite herself Isobel's interest was piqued. She'd always loved old cars.

But Rafael had come around to open her door and was waiting for her, hand outstretched. Thoughts of anything else disappeared. Isobel had no choice but to take his hand, and hated the tingle of awareness that raced up her arm, the inevitable blooming of heat.

Staff in pristine black-and-white uniforms were waiting for them at the top of the steps. They blurred and morphed into a jumble of names and faces as Rafael introduced them all. As soon as the introductions were made they scattered, and only a housekeeper was left to guide them into the house. Isobel remembered her name: Juanita. And also the fact that she looked none too friendly.

Rafael turned to Isobel. 'Come, I'll show you to your room, where you can freshen up. The guests will be arriving at the back of the property, where a wedding marquee has been erected for the reception.'

Isobel ignored his outstretched hand this time, and followed him slowly up the stairs. To her surprise the walls weren't hung with stern portraits of ancestors. Instead there were modern works of art which she guessed weren't copies.

Despite herself she asked, a little breathlessly as she tried to keep up in her long gown, 'Is this your family home?'

Rafael waited at the top of the stairs, hands in pockets and looking so rakishly handsome that Isobel had to cling onto the banister. He shook his head, 'No. My family home is in Barrio Norte—again not far. I bought this about ten years ago.'

'Oh…' Isobel climbed the last few steps and followed Rafael as he led her down a wide, luxuriously carpeted corridor. At the end he indicated two doors which were facing each other.

He opened the door on the left and led the way in to reveal a suite of rooms. 'They're two identical suites, both with bedrooms, bathrooms and dressing rooms.'

Isobel guessed this was his domain by its dark colours and unashamedly masculine furnishings. She was too bemused to feel anything else at the moment, and followed him to another door, through a sitting room which had a state-of-the-art audio-visual system.

This door led into another sitting room, a mirror image of the first, albeit in softer, more neutral tones.

He turned to face her. 'I appreciate that this has all moved quite fast, Isobel, and I'll respect your need for some space and privacy at the start of our marriage. While I do expect you to share my bed, I won't expect you to take up the more traditionally intimate role of sharing my rooms until you're ready.'

Spots danced before Isobel's eyes, and the fire in her veins was starting to bubble threateningly. But Rafael had already moved on and was heading for the bedroom. Isobel stomped after him, holding up her dress.

She walked in to see him standing at the open door of a dressing room, and when she looked she saw that every surface, nook and cranny was filled to overflowing with a wardrobe of clothes and shoes. Her own tatty luggage stood still packed in a corner, as if someone had deemed it not even worth unpacking.

Her jaw dropped. She walked closer.

'Consider it your trousseau,' Rafael said easily, as she looked in horror at row upon row of undoubtedly designer-label clothes. Her skin crawled with the sensation that he'd bought her, like some sort of living, walking doll.

She rounded on Rafael, white with fury boiling over. 'How *dare* you?'

His jaw tightened. 'How dare I what, Isobel? Provide for my wife?'

Isobel was shaking. 'How dare you presume to buy me a wardrobe full of clothes that will go to waste? I don't wear designer outfits. How dare you presume to think that I'll just fall into your bed, and how dare you presume to patronise me and give me *my space* until such time as I'm ready? Well, I'll tell you something now. I'll *never* be ready, and as for—'

Her words were stopped when Rafael's mouth came crashing down on hers, his arms tight around her. Isobel's hands were fists crushed against his chest, trying to push him back. The same inevitable reaction was pooling in her body and between her legs, but this time she knew what it was and fought it with all her strength, even though she ached to just sink and give in. She couldn't. Too much was at stake.

She stiffened and shut her mouth in a tight line against Rafael's sensual ministrations. He seduced and cajoled, and after torturous seconds Isobel found her resolve weakening under a welling of need. To her utter disgust and chagrin her body was betraying her again, softening, ripening, opening, instinctively wanting to allow this man access.

Rafael's mouth gentled, and when he took it away Isobel's head fell back. She sucked in a breath when she felt his mouth press hotly where her pulse throbbed at the base of her neck.

Big hands moulded her body, skimmed over curves, and her wedding dress felt constrictive. Without knowing how he'd managed it, Isobel felt something soft at the back of her legs, and suddenly the world was tipping. She fell back onto the bed in an ungainly sprawl. Shock and mortification washed through her in waves at seeing a still pristine Rafael standing looking down at her. She struggled inelegantly to sit up, hampered by the dress and her own sense of disorientation.

He flicked a look to the open dressing room. 'There is no negotiation on the wardrobe. You'll wear those clothes if I have to dress you myself. I will not be made a laughing stock in public because you insist on wearing the kind of bargain basement dresses you got away with in Paris.'

Isobel could feel that her veil had come off somewhere, and more waves of humiliation rose up as she rested back on her hands, still unable to stand up from the bed, seriously afraid her legs wouldn't hold her up.

She opened her mouth, but Rafael cut her off brutally. 'I could have these rooms stripped bare in a few hours and insist that you move into mine today, but I will extend you the benefit of the doubt for now and assume that you are merely coming to terms with your new life.'

He bent down and came close, snaked a hand around Isobel's neck. The skin of his hand burned against her bare skin.

'And, yes, Isobel, you *will* fall into my bed—whenever and however I want. We've just proved that you want me just as much as I want you. However, I think your lack of experience will make restraint for you harder to bear…'

Isobel knocked his hand away, but more because he was ready to let her go than because of her strength—and that made her even angrier. To her intense relief he stood up and moved back a few feet. She sat up. 'Don't believe that you know everything, Rafael. Just because I didn't have a boy-friend in Paris it does not mean I didn't have lovers.'

Right now, the thought of him suspecting she was still a virgin made her clammy with horror. Would he think that she'd waited for him? *Had she on some level waited for him?*

She went even clammier and did her own impression of raking her eyes up and down his body, tried to inject as much disdain into her voice as possible. 'Perhaps I've not had the indiscriminate quantity of *your* experience, but quantity does not always equal quality.'

Rafael stepped back and chuckled dangerously. For the first time in long minutes Isobel felt as if she could breathe again.

'I'll leave you to freshen up. And you might want to put on a little make-up to take down that flush in your cheeks. People will suspect that we've been getting a head start on our wedding night.'

He calmly and insouciantly walked to the door and then turned back. 'The photographer will be ready soon, so when you come down we'll get the photos out of the way. I'll be waiting downstairs.'

He left and closed the door behind him. Isobel picked up a pillow from the bed and threw it at the door, where it bounced ineffectually back onto the carpet. Which was exactly how she felt—*ineffectual*.

Knowing it was useless, but wanting to do something, Isobel hauled herself off the bed and went to the interconnect-ing door to their rooms, her dress swishing around her feet. She locked it, relishing the sound it made. Unfortunately, it gave only the merest hint of a veneer of security. Rafael couldn't be locked out for ever, and she was very much afraid that he'd already found a way into a place within her that had no lock and key.

Going into her new bathroom didn't help matters. Rafael had been right. She was flushed and her eyes were overbright. Her mouth was slightly swollen and pink from his kiss. With a cry of disgust, Isobel splashed her face with cold water and went to find her make-up bag so that she could eradicate the damage. The awful thing was, she knew if Rafael hadn't stopped when he had they might well be on their way to consummating this marriage—virginity or no virginity.

Rafael stood at the window of his study and looked out over the lush expanse of lawn to where he could see guests already walking up the pathway to the beautifully decorated marquee. He could hear the faint strains of music. Waiters greeted the guests with glasses of sparkling vintage champagne. The wedding had taken place in the late afternoon so the sun was starting to set, staining the sky in a dusky mauve colour.

As soon as the light dipped further the fairy lights strung in the trees would come on, along with flaming lanterns.

It was a perfect wedding. It was exactly as Rafael had envisaged it happening. He realised something in that moment. Despite his lack of choice in the matter, he knew that Isobel was right for him. He felt it deep in his bones; it was what he'd sensed three years before. And he also felt it in a more strategic part of his anatomy, which was still hot and hard. It had taken more restraint than he'd thought he possessed not to follow her down onto that bed and take her there and then, up in her bedroom.

He recalled her as she'd stood in front of him, just before he'd kissed her, her chest rising and falling rapidly. Hands balled into fists. Veil askew. Spitting like a cornered cat. And he could not remember ever being so blindsided by lust for a woman. He'd been unable to stop himself from hauling her into his arms. And to feel the way she'd put up her resistance and then melted into him so deliciously, kissed him so passionately, the way no novice could possibly kiss—it had sent some welcome sanity into his hot and tangled brain.

She was artful, and she knew exactly what she was doing. He was used to manipulative women. He'd learnt at the hands of one of the best: his ex-fiancée.

She'd all but admitted up there that she was no virgin, so her shy little moves and blushes were just an act, designed to bring him to the edge of his control. And he had no doubt that once she'd brought him to that edge she'd drive him back again. Teasing him to show him that she was in control. Did she have some plan to drive him into another woman's arms so that she might even initiate a divorce?

His mouth firmed. He wouldn't let her get away with this. The ultimate triumph would be his when she lay underneath him, panting and sobbing for him to take her.

A knock sounded on the door and he turned to see a paler, albeit still slightly mutinous-looking Isobel standing on the threshold. 'Juanita told me where to find you. The photographer is waiting outside. He says the light is falling…'

Schooling his features, and fighting the surge of lust which nearly blindsided him again at the sight of her, Rafael strode to his new wife and reassured himself that once she was tamed they would have a very nice life indeed. He took her by the arm and said sanguinely, 'I'd better make the most of your cooperative mood.'

CHAPTER FIVE

A FEW hours later Isobel knew that it was sheer grit keeping her from collapsing in a heap. Her face was numb from smiling, her hand aching from shaking hands. And at every step of the way Rafael was at her side, carrying her along. After the photographs had been taken, with her parents and his mother, who had seemed friendly enough, Rafael had led Isobel and her parents back into his study, where their respective lawyers had been waiting.

There, the basic and sordid reality of their marriage had hit home. Hard. It had been nearly too much to take in—to think that this deal had been born out of her grandfather's desperation to save the *estancia* at all costs, and Rafael's father's manipulative machinations.

Rafael had presented a cheque for an astronomical amount of money to Isobel's parents, and they'd signed a contract to say that the deal was now closed, all terms and conditions met.

Isobel had been disgusted by her parents' unashamedly avaricious response. They were seeing only the dollar signs of their inheritance coming their way at last, and not the fact that their only daughter was being forced into a marriage she didn't want. She'd felt intensely alone.

One of the women who had helped Isobel into her dress

earlier in the day had appeared as they'd come out of the study and taken her upstairs, where she'd taken off her veil and shown her a little wrist-tie on the train of the dress so she could keep the dress up and out of her way while she danced with Rafael for the traditional first dance.

Not knowing what to expect for that first dance, she'd been surprised when Rafael had spoken to the band and then started the crowd clapping rhythmically to the music of 'La Chacarera,' a traditional Argentinian folk dance. He'd taken off his jacket and tie, opened the top button of his shirt, and he looked so rakishly handsome that for a second Isobel had felt seriously overwhelmed.

Her chest had felt tight. She'd always found the simple dance impossibly romantic, its trademark being the intense eye contact between the man and the woman as they circled each other, with arms held high, turning without touching in a mesmeric series of back-and-forth steps to the beat of the music. It was a game of advance and retreat, and Isobel couldn't help but feel that it mirrored how she felt about Rafael, being alternately drawn to him and wanting to get as far away as possible.

The truth was she couldn't have broken eye contact even if she'd wanted to, and there had been something incredibly intimate about it. Eventually, when Rafael had caught Isobel into him at the end, and everyone had clapped raucously, he'd just said, *'I've got you now...'* And it truly did feel as if he had caught her, for good.

The band had switched to a different number then, to Isobel's intense relief. The dance had had a more profound effect on her than she cared to admit.

Now, Isobel felt a little removed from everything. The fact that she was the joint owner of her grandmother's estate still hadn't fully sunk in. Nor the fact that her parents would not have to worry about money for a long time, if ever again. Nor the fact that she was now married to the man who'd made countless women stare at her jealously all evening. She wanted to shout at them the truth of her sham marriage and tell them that they were welcome to him. But the fact was not one of them would *expect* that their marriage was anything more than arranged. Two great families coming together. Strategically sharing assets. *Love?* People would guffaw at the thought.

And then the tiny hairs stood up on the back of Isobel's neck. It was the extra-sensory response that was becoming annoyingly familiar whenever Rafael had left her side for longer than a few minutes. She saw him approach her through the crowd, another tall, dark man by his side. It was only when they drew closer that she could see the startling resemblance; they were both breathtakingly handsome. Rafael confirmed her suspicions.

'Isobel, I'd like you to meet Rico Christofides—my older brother.'

Isobel held in a gasp of recognition. She'd had no idea that the legendary Greek industrialist was Rafael's half-brother. They were similar in many ways, mainly in height and build, but where Rafael's eyes were dark, Rico's were a steely-grey. And unnervingly direct. There was something unbearably harsh about his features and it surprised her, as in comparison it made Rafael seem a little softer. That made her belly quiver. She didn't want to think of Rafael as soft. The man she'd read about in the papers was not soft.

She held out her hand. 'Pleased to meet you.'

'Likewise.' He shook her hand, and Isobel felt nothing at his cool, impersonal touch. This brother did not have the same cataclysmic effect on her. Isobel was almost disappointed—

as if she'd wanted some reassurance that Rafael's touch *wasn't* uniquely disturbing to her equilibrium.

'Business in Europe delayed me, so I couldn't make the church.' His voice was deep and attractively accented, but nevertheless it, too, had little effect on Isobel. All Rafael had to do was say her name and her bones melted.

Rafael had come round to pull Isobel into his side. She automatically stiffened against his possessive hold. 'It's nice that you could make it to the reception.'

Rico sent a mockingly amused glance to Rafael. 'I congratulate you both and wish you luck, but don't expect a reciprocal visit to *my* wedding any time soon. I won't be so easily caught.'

Isobel all but rolled her eyes at this further evidence of the insufferable arrogance running in the family. She elbowed Rafael in the ribs when he moved to pull her closer, and smiled sweetly at Rico. 'Oh, believe me, after today I'm over weddings myself.'

Rico tipped his head back and let out a shout of laughter, before shaking his head and saying to Rafael, 'I think you may have met your match, little brother.'

Their mother came along then to greet her oldest son, and a very definite tension spiked the air between the three of them. Isobel guessed that while Rafael and Rico undoubtedly got on and respected each other, there was a slight uneasy wariness between them, too, and she found herself wondering about their history, about who Rico's father was, and if that was why he hadn't taken over the Romero business.

After a few minutes of conversation Rafael's mother made her excuses, pleading tiredness, and left. A lot of the guests had already left, too, and Rico had drifted away to talk to a stunningly beautiful woman.

Rafael followed her look and said tightly, 'I wouldn't go there, if I were you. My brother has a notorious reputation.'

Isobel snorted delicately and looked up at Rafael, trying not to let his sheer dynamism affect her. But already she felt a little breathless. 'No more notorious than you.'

He came round in front of her and lifted her hand to his mouth, pressing a kiss against it. 'Ah, but now I'm a reformed, happily married man who has eyes only for his wife.'

Everything about him was mocking, but still Isobel couldn't help a quiver of longing rushing through her. She was so disgusted with her reaction that she ripped her hand from his. 'I'm quite tired now. I think I'd like to go to bed.'

Rafael's eyes smouldered. 'My thoughts exactly.'

Panic flared. *'Alone.'*

Rafael's face went stony-hard; his eyes turned to black. In that moment Isobel amended her previous thought that he wasn't as harsh as his brother. Now they could be twins.

'You are my wife, Isobel, and we will be sleeping together. This will be a proper marriage—in bed and out. Now, are you going to come and say goodnight to our guests and walk out of here like the dignified woman that you are? Or are you going to make me put you over my shoulder? Either way, I don't think the spectators would be disappointed. The latter option would give us a nice romantic edge and keep the coffee mornings buzzing for a few days. It's up to you.'

Isobel tipped up her chin and looked at Rafael coolly, belying her nervousness. 'You don't have to carry me anywhere like Tarzan.'

'Pity,' he drawled, 'I was hoping you'd give me an excuse.'

Within minutes he'd led Isobel around the wedding marquee as they made their goodbyes to the remaining guests—including his brother, Rico, who now had the beautiful woman clinging to him like a limpet and looking as if she'd just won a lottery ticket worth millions. The avaricious glitter in her eyes was unmistakable.

In that moment Isobel caught a glimpse of how a man like Rafael could grow cynical. And then, with her hand caught firmly by Rafael's, he led her through the moonlit garden and into the house. Panic was like a frantic caged bird beating against her breastbone as they drew closer and closer to the bedroom doors.

Rafael opened his door, and then turned and picked Isobel up into his arms so fast that her breath caught and she felt dizzy. 'What are you doing?'

As if she weighed nothing, Rafael said, 'Carrying you over the threshold.' And he did just that, before putting her back on her feet on the other side. His bed loomed large and threatening through the door of the bedroom, just feet away. Rafael kicked the door closed.

Isobel backed away and watched as Rafael started to open his shirt, to reveal the start of a bronzed chest, a few whorls of dark hair. She put up a hand, panic strangling her voice. 'Wait—stop.'

Rafael's fingers halted on his buttons. Intense irritation spiked through the burn of desire rushing through his blood. All he could see was Isobel, standing before him, her pale shoulders bare, gleaming in the dim light. The delicate swells of her breasts were tantalisingly visible just above the bodice of her dress. Something caught his eye, and he looked down to see her twisting her hands.

He breathed deep, sensing a delay in having his needs met. His suspicion that his new wife was playing the game of a tease made him grind out, 'Isobel? What is it?'

The confidence and fiery bravado that he'd become used

to was gone, and suddenly she looked very young. Through the make-up he could see dark shadows under her eyes, and something clenched in his gut. But he quashed it. She was acting. That was all. Testing her control over him. He was certainly not about to let her see how much he wanted her.

Isobel bit her lip, her eyes darting to Rafael and then away again. More concerned than irritated now, despite himself, he said, 'Isobel—'

She blurted out, 'I just…I really want to go to bed alone. This has all happened so fast, and I've barely even seen you since we came back to Argentina. Two weeks ago I was living in Paris and yet here I am… It's a lot to take in.'

Isobel forced herself to look at Rafael, her hands wringing together even tighter, knuckles showing white. She couldn't do this—couldn't just let him take her to bed like this. For so many reasons—not the least of which was her response to him, and how much it confused her, and how she had to get it under some kind of control so that she could cope. But right now she couldn't. And she was terrified he'd touch her and scramble all her thoughts. He'd done that in the church earlier with his kiss. And then when he'd kissed her again in her bedroom she'd very nearly lain back and given herself up completely.

Rafael just looked at her, his face unreadable in the shadows of the dark room. Eventually he let out a breath and ran a hand through his hair. Tension vibrated off him in waves, enveloping Isobel.

'I'm not in the habit of forcing unwilling women into my bed, Isobel, and I've no intention of starting now with my wife. Please, by all means, go to your own bed.'

Isobel looked at him warily, suspicion coiling deep within her that he was giving in too easily. There had been an element to his voice she hadn't missed but couldn't place—almost as if he wasn't entirely surprised. He'd stuffed his hands into his pockets, and his face was as blank as before, but a muscle twitched in his jaw.

Sensing that she was on a very short leash, Isobel backed away towards the connecting door. 'Thank you.'

But when she reached it she realised that it was still locked from when she'd locked it earlier. Flushing with embarrassment, she stalked back and past Rafael to go out through his main door, and heard his softly mocking, 'You really don't need to lock me out, Isobel. Soon enough you'll be welcoming me with open arms.'

Isobel's hand was on the knob, and her heart hammered when she heard Rafael call her name. Back straight, she tensed even more when she realised he was right behind her. Panic nearly made her sway. Had he changed his mind?

She started to turn around, to plead if she had to, but every word died on her lips when she felt his hands at the top of the back of her dress. She couldn't move.

'I don't think you're going to be able to get out of that by yourself…let me help.'

Speechless, and feeling as though she was burning up from the inside out, she felt Rafael take the zip and slowly pull it down—all the way until the knuckles of his fingers touched the bare, sensitive skin just above her buttocks. She still had a hand on the knob of the door, and her other hand held the now gaping dress to her chest. Burning all over, she managed a strangled sound of something vaguely coherent and pulled the door open.

All she heard as she fled to her own room was a soft, dark chuckle. She shut her bedroom door behind her, resting against it for a long moment before a curiously unsatisfied ache down low in her abdomen registered. It was an ache that she didn't want to think about, and she resolutely ignored it as she undressed and crawled into bed.

The morning came with a somewhat rude awakening: the sound of a tray banging down by Isobel's bed. She sat up in a panic, not knowing for a second where she was. It all came flooding back, though, when she saw the sour features of Juanita as the housekeeper drew back the heavy curtains and allowed sunlight to flood the room.

'Good morning,' Isobel said faintly.

Juanita all but ignored her, turning at the door to say curtly, 'Your husband is in the dining room. He is waiting for you.'

And then she was gone. On the tray that Juanita had delivered was a glass of orange juice. As much as Isobel would have liked to ignore the summons, she was wary of antagonising Rafael.

After a quick shower, and dressing in her own jeans and a faded check shirt, she went downstairs, bringing the tray down with her. She found the dining room when she saw Juanita emerge through a heavy oak door. The housekeeper barely acknowledged Isobel, just took the tray and gestured with her head to the door.

Isobel went in and saw Rafael's impressive back facing her. She slipped into the seat to his right, at the head of the table, and tried to ignore the way butterflies had erupted to life in her belly. If she'd been more in control of herself perhaps they would really be man and wife now, in every sense of the word.

He was reading a paper and sipping coffee from a small cup which should have looked ridiculous in his huge hand, but didn't. Isobel avoided his eye and shook out her napkin.

'Good morning.' She reached for a fluffy-looking croissant. 'I think your housekeeper has it in for me.'

Rafael tutted and shook his paper. 'Nonsense. She's just a romantic at heart, and I don't think she's under any illusions as to the nature of our marriage.'

His voice was dry. He was clearly referring to their separate beds last night. He turned back to his paper, leaving Isobel seething with a tumultuous mix of emotions in her breast. She took a bite out of her croissant and chewed disconsolately. It had looked so delicious, but now it tasted like sawdust.

After a couple of minutes' silence, Rafael put down the paper and fixed those dark eyes on her. She couldn't look away.

He ran his eyes over what she was wearing and Isobel flushed. 'I knew I should have told Juanita to dispose of your own clothes.'

Isobel gasped, but before she could say anything, Rafael continued.

'We're leaving for our honeymoon in a couple of hours. I'll have Juanita pack for you. I told you before, Isobel—I won't have you making a mockery of me and our marriage.'

'Honeymoon?' Trepidation laced Isobel's voice as visions of deserted beaches and vast villas and just the two of them flooded her mind. Trepidation and something much scarier.

Rafael grimaced. 'Don't worry. I'm not enough of a masochist to seclude us on a desert island just yet. I thought you might like to see the Estancia Paradiso, and I could do with catching up on things. I haven't been there in a couple of months…'

Isobel felt a little winded, and then all sorts of nebulous feelings rose up. What could she say? She'd love to see the *estanica*. 'Well… That is, of course I'd like to see it.'

A tug of nostalgia for her grandparents made her look

away to concentrate on her plate. He was surprising her. She'd fully expected to wake up today and have an empty house welcome her. Her parents had always maintained a good distance in their marriage, meeting only for stilted dinners in the evening and agonising social events where they and many other couples like them projected a false image of unity.

After a few minutes Rafael excused himself to get his things ready and left Isobel sitting there, still dazed. On automatic pilot she got up and started to clear the table, but Juanita came in and tutted.

'You don't have to worry about that,' she said.

Still not a glimmer of friendliness. Isobel said firmly, 'Fair enough. But you don't have to pack for me, Juanita. I can do that myself.'

The woman just nodded her head and busied herself clearing the table. Isobel went upstairs. She looked wistfully at her own bag of clothes, but remembered Rafael's threat that he would dress her himself. She shivered and reluctantly started to go through the clothes in the closet. To her surprise she found that most of the clothes weren't too far off the mark from what she would have chosen herself.

Wondering uncomfortably if Rafael had been involved with picking out the wardrobe, she changed into a pair of cargo pants and a classic white shirt. She couldn't forget that here in BA they were in the middle of winter. Even if the temperature didn't drop the same way it did in Europe, there was still a nip in the air.

When she came downstairs with her bag, an older smiling man took it out to where a luxury Range Rover waited. Isobel wandered out and breathed deep, and then spotted something that had piqued her interest before. The vintage cars parked up in one corner of the huge forecourt.

She walked over, her pulse quickening at seeing one in particular. She walked around it and touched it reverently.

'It's a 1951 Bugatti.'

Isobel jumped minutely. How did Rafael do that? Creep up on her when he was such a big man? She looked at him warily and took in properly that he was dressed in jeans and a casual shirt. Her pulse sped up, and it had nothing to do with the car. She looked away, willing down the heat that threatened upwards.

'I know. There are only eight in the world.' And each one was worth the equivalent of the national debt of a small country.

He quirked a brow. 'I'm impressed. You like vintage cars?'

Isobel nodded, focusing on the sleek and gorgeous lines of the car. 'I got it from my grandfather. He was fanatical about them. He always coveted one of these—he showed me pictures in a magazine.' Isobel smiled wryly. 'I used to promise him that when I grew up I'd make enough money to buy him one. I was only about twelve.'

'You could now…but it's too late.'

Isobel smiled sadly. 'Yes.' She looked at Rafael and her breath caught at the look in his eyes.

'Your grandfather sounds like he was an interesting man.'

Isobel fought his seductive pull valiantly. She had no doubt he was just turning on the charm, and was no more interested in her grandfather than in the inner workings of her mind. She was a challenge to him, that was all. And thinking about her grandfather was making her feel far too emotional.

'He was.' She cut off any further line of enquiry, and could see Rafael's jaw clench in response. Ridiculously, she felt guilty.

He stepped back and gestured to the Range Rover with his arm. 'We'd better get going. It's a four-hour drive and I want to get there before it gets dark.'

* * *

Still feeling wrong-footed as Rafael expertly negotiated the heavy Buenos Aires traffic, Isobel was taken aback when he asked casually, 'Where did you learn how to tango?'

She shot him a look, but he was facing forwards. After a long moment, her fingers plucking at her trousers, she said, 'My grandparents both loved it. My grandmother started teaching me when I was tiny, and then after she died my grandfather used to dance with me…' She snuck another glance at him, curiosity getting the better of her. 'You said in Paris that your grandmother used to take you and your brother to *milongas*?'

Rafael cast her a quick look and quirked a small smile, making Isobel's breath hitch. 'She was crazy about it—even though when she was growing up tango was still not considered entirely appropriate for her class. She used to sneak us into *milongas* and get her friends to teach us.'

Isobel nodded. 'For my grandparents it was the same, but they used to dance it anyway—usually when they were alone. So that's how you know the old *milonguero* style…like my grandfather?'

He nodded.

Isobel sat back and looked out of the window. She could feel her guard dropping, although a part of her couldn't believe it was so easy to talk to Rafael like this. 'I used to watch them dance. I thought it was the most beautiful thing I'd ever seen…' She smiled faintly. 'I can remember feeling like such a voyeur— as if I was intruding on something incredibly intimate.'

Dry humour laced Rafael's voice when he said, 'Where you saw white picket fences springing up, with roses around doorways and true love, all I saw was a way to impress beautiful girls… You really are just a romantic at heart, aren't you, Isobel?'

Isobel shot him a withering look and crossed her arms. She

faced away and shut her eyes on his far too amused face by pretending to go to sleep.

She woke to a gentle shake and her name being called with a seductively husky voice. 'Isobel…wake up. We're here.'

Isobel sat up to see Rafael move back. She felt exposed at having slept so easily beside him, and in her sleep she could see that she'd gravitated towards him. She moved a hand through her hair, ruffling the short silky strands, feeling disorientated. 'Did I sleep the whole way?'

Rafael nodded, his eyes intense on her. 'Pretty much. Once we hit the outskirts of Buenos Aires you were gone.'

'I'm sorry…' Isobel said stiffly, coming more awake. 'You must be tired, too.'

Rafael quirked an incredulous brow. 'Concerned, Isobel?'

Thankfully, Isobel saw some people approach the car and Rafael turned and got out before he could make sense of what Isobel couldn't make sense of herself. A smiling man opened her door and she got out, smiling back.

It was only then that she noticed where they were, and the stunning surroundings, and the fact that she was breathing in clean, pure air. Rafael was instructing staff to carry their bags in, but Isobel was frozen, a wave of *déjà vu* washing over her.

He came to stand beside her, where she was looking at the mountains in the distance.

'We're in the foothills of the Sierras Chicas. Do you remember it?'

Isobel shook her head. 'Barely. I only came here a couple of times when I was small. I think my mother always felt it was too far out of Buenos Aires. And then my grandmother died when I was six, and we never came back.' She looked at Rafael. 'That must have been when my grandfather sold it.'

He nodded. 'It was a couple of years after that.'

It struck Isobel forcibly in that moment just how long ago their fate had been decided. Avoiding Rafael's penetrating look, she turned around and gasped as she took in the sheer understated elegance and beauty of the *estancia*. Cream walls and a terracotta-tiled roof made it look warm and inviting. The one-level storey was very traditionally colonial, and the columns gave it an air of grandeur.

'It dates from the eighteen-thirties, but has been added to over the years…' Rafael pointed to an extension which looked slightly out of sync with the rest of the building, but still worked somehow. 'That's a neo-classical Italian addition, probably from around the late eighteen hundreds.'

'It's beautiful.' Isobel's voice was husky. 'I'd forgotten how beautiful it is.'

The land around the house was verdant and lush. Isobel could see what looked like a lake surrounded by trees towards the back of the *estancia*. She felt a wave of sadness then, at knowing that they'd lost this for so many years. No wonder her grandfather had wanted to make sure this returned to them eventually. She could see how losing this must have pushed him even closer to despair.

'And it's now yours as much as mine.'

Isobel felt tongue-tied. The enormity of the reality of her situation overwhelmed her for a moment. Luckily Rafael didn't seem to expect her to say anything, and started to stride towards the house with loose-limbed grace. Isobel forced herself to move and follow him when he said, 'Come on. I'll show you around.'

Her head was reeling about an hour later when Rafael led her back into the impressive reception area. Twenty-three bedrooms. Two private suites. A dining room fit for royalty…and kitchens that would put a five-star hotel to shame. One formal living area and a more informal one, complete with TV, sound system and shelves heaving with books.

Unaware of Isobel's inner meltdown, Rafael was striding out through the main door again, beckoning her to follow him. She followed him back to the car speechlessly and got in when he held the door open. They drove down a rough path hidden in the undergrowth by the side of the house and came out into a large clearing, where a helicopter stood waiting.

Isobel was seriously afraid she wouldn't be able to process much more, but already Rafael was at her door and helping her out. The helicopter was starting up.

'I thought this might be the best way to give you an idea of the estate. We have some time before it gets dark.'

Within what felt like seconds they were in the helicopter and lifting into the air. It was Isobel's first time, and her hands gripped the armrests. She was connected to Rafael via headphones and speakers, and as they flew over the fifty-thousand-hectare estate he pointed out the polo grounds and the stables, the livestock area, and where the land had been turned over to agricultural use. It went on and on and on, no end in sight.

Isobel was feeling more and more nauseous. Not helped when Rafael looked at her sharply and said, 'Are you okay?'

All Isobel could do was shake her head numbly. Rafael gave a signal to the pilot and the helicopter started to turn around and head back. As soon as they landed Isobel clambered out of the small craft and staggered slightly.

Rafael caught up to her and took her arm. 'What's wrong?'

At first Isobel couldn't get any words out. She was terrified she'd throw up there and then. She sucked in big breaths, feeling clammy and sweaty all at the same time. 'I just… It's a bit much to take in.' The enormity of the disparity between her simple life in Paris and her life here now was overwhelming.

When Isobel emerged from her room a little later her belly was still in knots. Thankfully, when a woman had shown Isobel to her room she'd seen that she wasn't expected to share with Rafael. But the evidence that he was sticking to his word wasn't making her feel any less threatened.

The woman appeared again, seemingly out of nowhere, and shyly took Isobel out to a terraced area at the back of the house. Isobel had put on loose-fitting wide trousers and a similarly loose top. She felt covered up and safe, unaware of how the luxuriousness of the fabric clung to her body provocatively.

Her trepidation spiked when she took in the nonchalant figure of Rafael, surveying his empire, hands in pockets, looking out over the beautiful lake at the bottom of the lush lawn. It suddenly hit home, in these beautiful and rarefied surroundings, that she was a trophy wife, joining her disgustingly powerful and wealthy husband for pre-dinner drinks, dressed to please him.

The scene was so reminiscent of what she'd witnessed growing up that Isobel felt nauseous for a second, because she knew how empty it was. A facade. And a part of her couldn't believe she hadn't tried harder to get out of it.

Rafael turned to face her then, and Isobel had to steel herself not to be distracted by him.

'Drink?'

She shook her head, and then changed her mind because her throat felt dry. 'A sparkling water, please.' What was it about this man that instantly reduced her to something so primal?

She accepted the glass, careful not to let their fingers touch, and took a deep gulp, moving so she too could look out on the view. That nausea seemed to grow inside her. She felt stiff and cold. She could see now how everything had fallen into place for him so easily. He'd decided he wanted a convenient wife, and a legal agreement had dictated it should be her. Rafael was happy because he had achieved the respectability and stability he needed. Isobel had nothing—not one atom of what she'd ever really wanted.

She could feel Rafael looking at her, and then he said tightly, 'It wouldn't kill you to smile, Isobel, and at least *look* like you're the happy bride.'

'What's the point?' she said in a brittle voice. She turned to look up at him. 'I mean, seriously, what's the point?' She waved a hand outwards. 'Who is going to see us here? I can understand back in Buenos Aires it might be necessary, but *who* cares here?'

She was growing more and more agitated as the reality of everything seemed to be hitting her all at once. The luxurious feel of her clothes against her skin chafed like a hair shirt.

Rafael's eyes flashed dangerously. 'I care, Isobel. I care about this marriage. I believe it can work, that we can be good together, but not if you walk around looking as if you're going to your own funeral all the time. This is your life now. You have to come to terms with that.'

Rafael looked down at the woman beside him and a violent need throbbed through him, hardening his body. She looked like a sexily tousled elf, all slim limbs and shadows and hollows. Her mouth was tight and tension radiated off her. It irked him how well he seemed to be able to read her when no other woman had inspired that ability within him...not even Ana, the one woman he had thought he'd loved. His mouth tightened at the thought of his ex-fiancée and the humiliation he'd suffered at her hands.

'I never asked for this,' Isobel said faintly now, mesmerised despite herself by Rafael's eyes.

His jaw clenched. 'Neither did I—or has that escaped your notice?'

Isobel's nausea surged again. Of *course* he wouldn't be married to her if he had a choice—no matter how conveniently things had worked out. Suddenly to think of him hating this as much as her, despite their very real reasons for needing to marry, was no comfort.

She tore her eyes from his and put down her glass of water jerkily. 'You could divorce me, Rafael. You won't want to stay married to me. You don't love me.'

Rafael grabbed her wrist in a burning hold and pulled her close to him again. 'Of course I don't love you. This has nothing to do with love. And you're wrong. I'm quite happy with my new wife. I told you before, we will not be getting divorced. So whatever little plan you have, you can forget it. Do you think that by teasing me, leading me on only to deny me at the last moment, I'll grow impatient enough to seek another woman's arms and give you grounds for divorce?'

Isobel was genuinely confused, and she couldn't understand the lancing pain she felt at the thought of him going to another woman. 'What are you talking about?'

His mouth was a grim line. 'I mean the way you look at me, with those big expressive eyes which tell me you want me. Only then you plead for *space*, as if you don't know what you're doing. You don't have that power over me. No woman does. The only reason you've been given space is because *I've* allowed it. We both know you go up in flames the minute I touch you.'

Isobel moved away jerkily, realising they were standing too close, but he wasn't relaxing his grip for one second. She couldn't speak. She felt breathless, completely distracted. What was he talking about? She wouldn't know how to tease a man if her life depended on it. She was caught again by Rafael's eyes, which glowed molten brown. She could see the flecks of green, enticing and mysterious.

'It's time to give up your romantic dreams, Isobel. I'm the only man you're going to be married to, so you'd be wise to invest your energy in me. Do you forget so easily that without our marriage your parents would be facing financial ruin and social ostracism?'

His words hit her like body blows, but before she could betray the soft, tender core of her that pulsed to a very secret beat that spoke of her deep desire to find true love, she pulled herself together. She hadn't needed Rafael to spell out in no uncertain terms that her chances of finding that kind of relationship were all but gone.

She finally ripped her wrist from his grip and glared up at him. 'You will never truly know me or have me, Rafael. You make me sick. You've been handed everything your whole life, been pampered and waited on hand and foot. I hate everything you represent, and I hate *you*! You think you can just snap your fingers and it will all fall into place. I could never fall in love with someone like you. And as for teasing—'

Isobel's words were cut off under Rafael's brutal kiss. His arms were around her like steel bands and she couldn't move, couldn't breathe. Slowly, though, her treacherous reaction to his touch started. She tried to remain stiff and unresponsive, but it was impossible. Especially when his mouth softened, broke away for a moment and then came back, firm and yet soft. Coaxing and seducing her to respond.

If Isobel had been offered all she wanted in that very moment she wouldn't have been able to articulate it. She was in Rafael's arms, and her world was quickly shrinking to the way he was making her feel. Things seemed to escalate with scary swiftness. His hand was spearing through her short hair, massaging her skull, his tongue sliding deep to duel with hers.

She could feel his other hand reach under her baggy top and explore upwards to the bare skin above her trousers, curving over her waist and hip. As if on cue her breasts tightened and swelled, hungry for his touch. Against his mouth Isobel's breath came quick and fast, as if she couldn't contain it.

His hand was finally there, cupping her breast, and then almost roughly he pulled down the lace cup of her bra and his thumb found her puckered nipple, sliding back and forth, making Isobel wrench her mouth away completely to suck in air. Her arms were locked around Rafael's neck, and she had no idea how or when she'd done that.

All she knew was that there was a fire in her blood and only one person capable of putting it out. She felt all at once slumberous and yet as energised as she'd ever felt. Rafael's dark eyes held her captive. His hand dropped from her head and reached down for her leg, lifting it up so that it hooked slightly around his waist. And then, with a big hand on her bottom, he pulled her right into him—into where she could feel the throbbing, hard heat of his arousal.

His other hand was still on her breast, teasing that aching, tingling tip. And then reality hit. The very hard reality of just how much she wanted him. How easily he'd seduced her.

Everything he'd just thrown at her had been true. She was weak. She had no control. Immediately, Isobel started to struggle, and struggled even harder when she saw the mocking look of triumph cross Rafael's flushed face. He dropped her leg and let her go. To Isobel's intense embarrassment, she could barely stand on two legs.

He reached behind him for his drink, which he had put down, and drained the glass in one gulp. He arched a dark brow. 'I rest my case, Isobel. The only reason we're not horizontal on that carpet right now with the door locked against interruption is because of me. Your control is just an illusion. And next time you try this game we won't be stopping.'

Isobel felt wrung out, utterly exposed. He thought she was playing with him? He couldn't be further from the truth. She was terrified that sleeping with him would crash through her already flimsy defences. The problem was, she only seemed to be able to come to her senses when things had already gone too far. And he was right. He'd just shown her exactly who wielded the control and it wasn't her.

'You kissed *me* just now. I never asked for it. I hate you, Rafael.' But her voice trembled and her conscience struck her, telling her that the person she really hated was herself, for not being able to resist him even though he embodied all the greed and excess of a world she never wanted to be a part of.

'You did ask for it—with those big expressive eyes, Isobel. Perhaps you need to work on hiding your true desires a little better.'

Isobel opened her mouth to refute his words, but just then a discreet cough sounded nearby, and they both looked around to see a uniformed man waiting. 'Señor and Señora Romero, your dinner is served. If you'd like to come through to the dining room…'

CHAPTER SIX

'YOU'RE wrong, you know.'

Isobel looked up from her dinner plate warily. She still felt a little sick to her stomach, but it was directed at herself for being so monumentally weak—exactly as Rafael had accused.

Rafael was not looking at her. He was cradling a half-finished glass of wine, looking into its ruby-red depths.

His mouth thinned. 'Although I can't deny I had a life of privilege, it was much the same as you had…'

Isobel winced inwardly. She *did* deserve that. She'd had no less a privileged upbringing than he. 'Rafael, I—'

He ignored her, continuing, 'My father, however, liked to play fast and loose on the stock market. A couple of times he lost almost everything, only to make it back within twenty-four hours. One of those times was after a tip your grandfather gave him, and my father—being the suspicious, resentful man he was—made sure he got his revenge. Hence the deal regarding the *estancia*. I think it sent my mother a little crazy. But from a young age my brother and I were aware of how fickle wealth was, how it could be taken away from you in seconds…'

Isobel was a little blindsided to hear this. She twisted her napkin in her hand and asked hesitantly, 'What happened to Rico's father?'

Rafael took a sip of wine and looked at her. His eyes were very dark and hard and seemed to bore right through her. No emotion.

'My brother's father was a rich Greek tycoon. He seduced our mother and disappeared back to Europe when she fell pregnant, not wanting to get tied down in marriage. In a bid to save her reputation a marriage was brokered between my parents. My father's family needed the status of being married into an elite family, and my mother needed to have her baby in wedlock.'

A muscle twitched in Rafael's jaw. 'However, once Rico was born, it was clear he was nothing like my fair father. It was too much for him to take, so he used to beat him. And then when I came along and took after our mother's darker colouring he beat me, too, irrationally believing that I could be anyone's son. When Rico was sixteen he took a belt to him. I was in the room, too, due to be next. He beat Rico so badly that Rico turned on him and beat him back. He told him that if he ever lifted a hand to me again he'd come back and kill him. Rico left that day and went to Europe to look for his father.'

Isobel gasped softly. 'But you must have been just—'

'Twelve years old. My father never touched me again after that day.'

Isobel's throat hurt. Remorse filled her. 'Rafael, I'm sorry for what I said... I had no right to assume anything.'

Rafael's face was stark. 'I'm telling you this now because we're man and wife and you should know these things, but I don't want to speak of it again.'

Isobel bit her lip and then said in a rush, because she had to know, 'But how can you of all people be happy with a marriage of convenience when you came from what you did?'

His eyes flashed at her for her impudence, but Isobel wouldn't back down. She was his wife and she deserved to know.

'I'm happy with a marriage of convenience precisely *because* I realised a long time ago not to look for love in a marriage. The only kind of marriage I want is a marriage just like this, where we both know where we stand, with no emotions in the way to cloud things. Just because our parents didn't provide us with good examples it doesn't mean that we can't forge a successful partnership based on mutual respect.'

His eyes held hers captive and Isobel quivered inwardly when he added throatily, 'And desire.'

Isobel knew right then that Rafael's threat hadn't been an empty one. The next time he touched her they wouldn't be stopping—no matter how much she denied what her body screamed for.

The following evening Isobel sat on the far bank of the small lake behind the house and sighed deeply. The sky was a glorious twilight-infused blue backdrop, and a full moon already hung low in the sky. Golden lights flooded out from the long windows at the back of the *estancia* and threw a glittering reflection on the still surface of the dark lake.

It was so magically beautiful that her heart ached. She still reeled from her conversation with Rafael last night. Things had got heated so quickly, and she hadn't been able to control her emotions *or* her mouth. Or her physical reaction. It was becoming rapidly clear that when Rafael touched her she went up in flames, and she was terrified of getting badly burnt in the process. He shouldn't have the ability to be touching her emotionally. But she knew he did and that was very scary. The only way she could protect herself would be to try and maintain her distance, even if ultimately she was unsuccessful.

She thought again of what he'd revealed about his childhood and her heart ached. And he'd obviously hated telling her... She wondered why he had—he didn't strike her as the kind of person who cared what people thought of him, and she knew for a fact that this information was not common knowledge, even though Rico had re-emerged on the other side of the world with another man's name.

It made her own largely sterile upbringing pale in comparison. She'd never been subjected to the virulent hatred or violence that he had. No wonder there had been that atmosphere between Rico, Rafael and their mother at the wedding. It was as if she was looking at Rafael through refracted glass now, seeing a dozen new images of him reflected back, and it scared her—because she suspected that the Rafael she'd got a glimpse of last night had the potential to do a lot of damage to her equilibrium.

She could see now where his intense ruthlessness came from. The need to amass great wealth at any cost—even at the cost of innocent people. Financial stability must mean everything to him. She still felt sick when she thought of his business ethics, but having got some insight into his family, she couldn't help but empathise in a tiny way and that felt very dangerous.

The rest of their dinner last night had been stilted, and Isobel had escaped as soon as she could. That morning the housekeeper had told her that Señor Romero would be out all day, inspecting the estate by helicopter and on horseback. The time alone hadn't served to give Isobel any sense of regaining control of her emotions. She'd been on edge all day.

She couldn't help the sensation of having been flayed inside, as if strips had been torn off her own tender inner body.

Just then a movement caught her eye, and her gaze snagged on the tall, powerful figure of Rafael emerging from the golden light of the house. Isobel shrank back, but knew logically that he couldn't possibly see her across the lake. Her body tightened in a far too familiar way as she drank him in almost hungrily. The broad strength in his shoulders tapered down to a lean waist and those long, long legs. Even from here she could see the unleashed power in his tautly muscled form. She could tell that he was tense, and the fact that she could do so spoke of a kinship that she felt deepening every day.

With extreme reluctance Isobel finally got up and made her way back to the *estancia*, feeling very much as if she were voluntarily walking into the lion's den.

Rafael waited in the lounge that evening for Isobel to come in for dinner. He took a sip of whisky and relished the burn of velvet-smooth liquid as it slipped down his throat.

The previous evening had left a bitter taste in his mouth all day; he hadn't been able to get Isobel's face out of his mind, nor the flash of something achingly vulnerable in her eyes when he'd spilled his guts. And when he'd set her back from him after kissing her senseless. He grimaced. Who was he kidding? He'd almost been senseless, too. He was the one who lacked any control. Within touching distance of Isobel he turned into something feral, and the way she consistently pushed him away sent him into orbit with frustration.

He couldn't fathom why on earth he'd felt compelled to share something with her that up until now had been between him, his brother and his deceased father. Nor how the sympathy in her liquid brown gaze had got him right between the eyes. So much so that he'd told her curtly that he wouldn't discuss it again.

His hand clenched around the glass as he stared unseeingly out through the open patio doors. Yesterday he'd teased her for being a romantic. She'd blushed and then scowled at him, showing none of the guile or finesse he was used to in that situation. He'd obviously hit on a nerve. How could she be so different? How could she want something that clearly didn't exist? A cottage with a white picket fence, two people living without a care in the world… It was ridiculous. It didn't exist.

At the hands of his father he'd learnt an early lesson not to expect love or support, and yet he'd revealed a mortifying streak of vulnerability and had foolishly thrown caution to the wind when Ana Perez had whispered lies in his ears about how much she loved him. She'd loved his money and his social status. Never again would he be so deceived. And he had the ultimate protection now, in the form of this marriage.

A sound came from behind him, and Rafael forced his tense muscles to relax. He turned around. Isobel stood in the doorway, and as soon as her image registered on Rafael's retina his blood ran hot in his veins.

But he just smiled urbanely, and saw her react as colour tinged her cheeks. He gestured for her to come in. 'Drink?'

Isobel walked in and immediately felt hot under the collar—literally. She'd instinctively covered herself up with an unflattering silk shirt, buttoned all the way to her neck, and now she felt ridiculous. As if clothes could protect her like armour around *this* man…

She nodded, that heat climbing up into her face. In comparison to her, Rafael looked cool as a cucumber. 'Water, please.'

Before he handed her the glass he took her hand, and Isobel jumped. She looked at him warily. His eyes were molten and dark.

'Let's call a truce for now. Try to get on. Give this a chance. I'm giving you space…'

His eyes dropped down her body, and to Isobel's mortification she could feel her breasts swell and peak into hard points against the silk of the voluminous shirt.

'But I warn you now that if you ever come before me dressed like this again I'll strip the clothes off you and redress you myself. Dressing like that only makes me want to uncover the secrets of your delectable body even more.'

Heat and fire rushed through Isobel, and she felt in serious danger of falling down. She pulled her hand free with an effort and nodded jerkily. 'Fine. A truce.' She lifted her chin. 'And I don't know what you're talking about. There's nothing at all wrong with what I'm wearing. It was part of the trousseau.'

Rafael growled. 'If that's the case, the stylist is getting sacked. I'm warning you, Isobel, don't push me. I'm prepared to give you your precious space, but only for a finite time…' He finally gave her the glass of water, lifting his own glass high. 'To a truce—and a long and successful marriage.'

With the utmost reluctance Isobel touched her glass to his and took a drink, thankful that she didn't choke.

The following morning at breakfast Isobel felt gritty-eyed after a restless night. Rafael, however, looked as fresh as a daisy.

'I thought you might like to come around the estate with me today—get a proper feel for it. We can go on horseback.'

Isobel could feel herself go pale at the thought of taking in all that expanse again, and she put down her coffee cup with a clatter. She darted a look to Rafael. 'I don't know if I'm—'

He cut her off. 'You're going to have to get to grips with it some time. I'm sorry for giving you such a whirlwind tour the first day. I can see how overwhelming it must have been. But perhaps this way it'll be a little more manageable.'

Isobel felt torn. Of course she wanted nothing more than to get to know the *estancia*—but an entire day alone with Rafael? She'd already avoided something like this the day before. But now…she had no excuse. Her cowardly heart beat fast. She nodded abruptly. 'Okay. That sounds nice.'

A couple of hours later, astride a huge horse, with a wide-brimmed *gaucho* hat on her head, following Rafael, she knew *nice* didn't do it justice.

Isobel couldn't help a burgeoning feeling of something scarily like joy from expanding her chest. And pride to know that everything in sight had belonged to her grandmother and was now partly hers again… Paris and the life she'd led there seemed like a far distant memory.

An assertion gripped her: she belonged here. It rushed through her blood, stunning in its intensity. Up till now she'd never had that feeling.

The pampas stretched out around her, and the Sierras Chicas rose majestically in the distance. A lump, unbidden, constricted her throat. Just then Rafael stopped his horse and looked back. He sat with easy grace in his saddle, lean and awe-inspiring. Faded jeans moulded to hard thigh muscles. Isobel gripped her reins hard. She'd been avoiding looking at him ever since she'd watched him swing all too lithely into his saddle.

He smiled. 'Do you want to give these boys their heads?'

Isobel just nodded, incapable of speech, and followed Rafael's lead as he spurred his horse into a trot, and then faster, into a full-on gallop. She could feel her own mount bristle and move restlessly, and, taking a deep breath, she urged her horse on until he too was cutting through the wind like a bullet.

It was exhilarating. Isobel hadn't ridden like this in years—bent low over her horse's back, feeling as though they were joined as one. She even pulled past Rafael, and felt a helpless gurgle of delighted laughter break out. But of course he didn't let her beat him for long, effortlessly catching up and taking hold of her reins to slow them both down.

When she got her breath back Isobel could see outbuildings, and Rafael explained that they were training grounds for the polo horses. A man on horseback came to meet them, and Rafael introduced him as Miguel Cortez, head trainer.

By the time the sun was setting that evening Isobel's head was spinning—but not in that sickly way it had the first day. It was buzzing with information. She'd found out that they hosted two world-class polo events there every year, and she'd looked at the plans Rafael had made to expand the grounds even further.

It was truly staggering. If her grandmother's estate had consisted of just the polo grounds, it would have been seriously impressive. But to know that the estate went on and included a livestock farm, and then an agricultural centre...

She shook her head now, trying to take it all in, looking into the distance. She felt Rafael come to stand beside her, and her body made its predictable response. She avoided looking at him; in this milieu, with his urbane surface stripped away, he was far too devastating. Right now he was nothing like the person she'd built up in her head—the cruel and ruthless businessman who had no qualms about entering into a loveless marriage of convenience, almost welcoming it. Hadn't he said that he was happy to be married to her? How was she supposed to fight *that?*

She felt unbearably confused. Up until now she'd always prided herself on being able to read people, but Rafael was proving to be quite the chameleon.

The pure joy she'd felt just a short while before made her too raw and exposed. As if she were betraying herself in some way. Her voice was husky. 'Thank you for showing me this.'

She could feel him shrug a broad shoulder in response. 'Like I keep saying, it's half yours, Isobel. I've asked the helicopter to meet us and take us back to the house. Tomorrow I'll show you the rest of the estate, and tomorrow night I've arranged for a barbecue at the house so that you can meet everyone.'

Isobel just nodded dumbly, her chest tight with conflicting emotions.

The following evening, back at the house, Isobel grimaced as she got out of the bath in her *en suite* bathroom. She ached all over from two days of being on horseback, but she couldn't deny an inner sense of peace and satisfaction. Her mind shied away from thinking too much about Rafael, and how patient he'd been—showing her everything, explaining how it all worked.

When she looked at herself in the mirror a little later she grimaced. She'd put on clean jeans and a soft silk blouse. Not wanting to attract Rafael's ire again, she opened up the first few buttons, having scary visions of him opening them for her if she buttoned up too much.

Her hair was still a little damp, but it would be dry within minutes. She emerged from her room and ran slap-bang into a wall of muscle. Rafael's arms came to hers, steadying her. Isobel looked up and couldn't move, her breath caught.

'I was just coming for you.'

'I know where the barbecue is, Rafael.' *Please move back— let me go*, she begged silently.

Rafael moved back, but Isobel didn't feel any safer.

'All the estate workers have come up for the barbecue. Do you think we can put on a united front for one night?'

Isobel shrugged, feeling hot. 'Of course. I mean…we are.'

He shook his head and folded his arms. 'Not when you flinch every time I come near you or jump like a scalded cat every time I touch you. We're meant to be on honeymoon, waking every morning in a tangle of bedsheets, limbs entwined and sated from passion spent.'

Isobel put out a hand, as if that might halt the flood of images his words had evoked like a lurid movie in her head. 'Fine—whatever. I'll pretend.'

He smiled smugly. 'Good.' He took her hand and Isobel fought not to jump, scowling when he said, *sotto voce*, 'It really won't be that hard.'

The following day, while Isobel waited in the Range Rover for Rafael to join her and drive them back to Buenos Aires, she closed her eyes with a feeling of desperation. Things were slipping out of her control completely. Last night she hadn't slept a wink, her entire body tingling after an evening spent with Rafael glued to her side, holding her hand or snaking an arm around her waist, pulling her into him so tightly that she had felt her breasts pressing into his hard chest.

She'd felt as if she was in a permanent state of heat. Waves of it washing over her. And every time she'd tried to escape he'd merely teasingly pulled her back and pressed a kiss to her brow—or, worse, once to her mouth—sending her pulse rocketing to space. When he did that it was so hard to try and remember why she had to keep her distance and protect herself, and she was certain he knew exactly what he was doing. After the barbecue, when he'd insisted on leading her back to her room, the gloating smile on his face had told her he'd enjoyed every minute of it.

Now the insufferable man was striding towards the car and Isobel had to bring up every defence she had left just to be able to look him in the eye. But when he got in, he took out his phone saying, 'I'm sorry—I've got to make this call.'

Isobel murmured something and felt a curious sensation of deflation. She half listened to a conversation that seemed to be with Rafael's PA in Buenos Aires. It had something to do with the big deal he was working on in the States, and reminded Isobel of his ruthless business dealings. She'd forgotten.

When he was finished he cut off the connection and said, 'I'm sorry about that. It was rude.'

Isobel shook her head, still feeling sick. 'It's fine. You've been away for a week. I can imagine there's a backlog of work.'

She felt Rafael slide her a glance, and saw him notice the rosewood box she had cradled on her lap.

'What's that?'

Isobel's hands tightened on it convulsively, as if protecting it. A little defensively she said, 'The housekeeper told me it belonged to my grandmother. There's something in it, but we couldn't find the key, so I'm going to try and open it in BA.' She sensed his curious look.

'Isobel, it's fine. It was your grandmother's. It's yours. You can do what you want with it.'

Isobel immediately felt wrong-footed and childish, and cursed herself. This man seemed to effortlessly bring out the worst in her, the most base part. She just said quietly, 'Thank you.'

'One of my assistants will be over this morning, with some credit cards and bank account details.'

Rafael was draining a cup of coffee, clearly getting ready to go to work. They were having breakfast in the informal dining room the morning after returning from the *estancia*. Already Isobel felt as if Buenos Aires was too loud and harsh, and she longed for the peace and tranquillity of the Estancia Paradiso again.

Rafael was a million miles from the relaxed man she'd spent a week with. He was dressed in a pristine suit, shirt and tie. Clean-shaven, hair slicked back. The industrial dragon in his element—back to business and sorting out the undesirables.

'But I have a bank account already,' Isobel pointed out, not wanting at that moment to have anything to do with his money.

Rafael shook his head. 'I've set up new ones for you. One of them holds the profit from the *estancia*—that's yours now, too.'

Panic clawed at her again. Did the man have no morals? 'But I can't spend the profits of the *estancia*. Surely that should go back into maintenance or wages or something?'

Rafael smiled a little patronisingly. 'It's the profit *after* all the maintenance and wages are looked after.'

Isobel's mind boggled. He hadn't been joking when he'd said it was a thriving business. 'Oh.' She looked at him. 'And what am I supposed to do now?'

He put his cup down. 'I told you already, Isobel, I'm not some gaoler. You can do what you want. Go shopping, meet friends, set up a charity for unwanted designer clothes—the world's your oyster now.' He stood up and loomed large over her. 'Why don't you take a few days to figure out how to spend your money? Go on a shopping spree. I can't imagine any woman turning that opportunity down.'

After a long week of disturbing and far too ambiguous emotions where this man was concerned, Isobel welcomed the rush of anger at this evidence of his sheer arrogance and his dismissive tone. She was back on ground she knew and understood.

She stood, too, and threw down her napkin. 'I have a room bigger than my entire apartment in Paris full of clothes upstairs. I have a vault full of jewellery. What on earth could I possibly want to buy? I've never shopped on the Avenida Alvear, and I'm not going to start now.'

And then, as if an internal demon had taken over, she couldn't stop. 'I'm used to going out to cafés for coffee with friends, talking about real issues. I'm used to doing my own shopping, not having it delivered to the house to be unpacked by a maid. I'm used to making my own meals, not being presented with *cordon bleu* dinners cooked by a Michelin-starred chef.' She finally stopped, breathing hard.

Rafael lifted his hands in a gesture of surrender, a definite hint of irritation lacing his voice. 'So go and find some kindred spirits and drink coffee all day, set the world to rights—or knock yourself out with grocery shopping. Or bake a cake. I really don't care, Isobel. This is your life now. You'd better get used to it.'

He turned to leave the room, took a few long steps, and then turned back, eyes flashing dangerously. 'And this is the other part of it—one of the primary functions of this marriage—be ready to go out to the opera at seven this evening. It's going to be our first public outing as a married couple.'

That evening Isobel was waiting, still seething. She'd seethed all day, and it had been made worse because she was very afraid that her anger had a lot to do with feeling betrayed by Rafael's morphing back to arrogant tycoon after showing her another side to him at the *estancia*, a more relaxed and charming side. The side of him which *should* have had her running for cover but which had seduced her all too easily, making her forget who he was.

Juanita, who was still as cool to Isobel as ever, saw her in the main reception room and huffed past the door. Isobel heard footsteps descend the main stairs and stood, then hurriedly sat down again, not wanting Rafael to see her so eager.

He came and filled the doorway, adjusting the cufflinks of his shirt. Dressed in a black tuxedo, he looked gorgeous.

He gestured with an imperious hand for Isobel to join him. Swallowing her anger, Isobel stood and walked over stiffly, trying to remain unmoved by his slow up and down appraisal.

He looked into her eyes as she came to stand before him. 'Beautiful. You're perfect, Isobel.'

'Well, I hope so. Because I spent all day today picking out the perfect dress so that I could be your perfect wife, Rafael. After all, you're sacrificing a hedonistic playboy existence for me, aren't you?'

Rafael felt a lance of hurt, and it made rage curl through him. He would *not* let his own wife get to him. He hadn't asked for or cared about anyone's opinion in a long time, and he wasn't about to start now. His uncharacteristic confession at the *estancia* would be the last time he explained himself to this woman.

His jaw clenched tightly and he snaked out a hand to take her chin and tip it up. 'Exactly. And do you know what would make things even more perfect? You coming into my bed. This waiting is growing tedious. I think you've had all the space one person needs, and the sooner that sharp tongue of yours has its edges smoothed by passion the better. All this sexual frustration really doesn't suit you—or me.'

CHAPTER SEVEN

IN THE back of his car Rafael shook with the effort it had taken not to haul Isobel into his arms in the house and kiss that mutinous mouth into submission. She was wearing a full-length gown in off-white, softly ruched and flowing, with a swathe of material over one shoulder, leaving the other bare. The material clung to her small, firm breasts, clearly outlining their alluring shape.

That morning, the prospect of day-to-day life with Isobel had hit home, and it hadn't been comfortable. He knew the sort of person she was: principled, and full of her own integrity. Of course she wasn't going to just seamlessly blend into the round of coffee mornings and lunches and shopping that most high-society wives filled their days with. So why had it rankled and pushed his buttons so much when he'd never really cared one way or the other for that scene, either?

He was afraid to acknowledge the fact that on some level, after the week at the *estancia*, he'd thought he could push Isobel back to some safe place, and yet she'd just come at him in her usual fashion, challenging and biting and hissing. Demanding that he see *her* and not put her in a neat box where he wouldn't have to deal with her. Which was exactly what he'd tried to do.

Isobel could feel waves of censure still emanating from Rafael, and felt acutely self-conscious in the fussy designer dress. She hitched up the strapless side, feeling too exposed, and nearly jumped a foot high when she felt Rafael's warm hand come onto her knee, sending a bolt of sensation straight between her legs.

'Stop fidgeting,' he growled.

He took Isobel's hand and lifted it up, forcing her gaze around his. She had to suck in a breath at the intensity in his dark eyes, and could see how his gaze moved down to her throat, where she could feel the beat of her traitorous pulse underneath her skin. A slow smile curved Rafael's sensual mouth and, aghast at the liquid pooling of heat in her belly, Isobel finally managed to wrench her hand away.

Rafael let her go, but didn't let her turn away from him. He brought a hand up to cup her jaw, the skin so silky-smooth and soft that he had to repress a groan of need. 'Remember our truce. We're in this together. We've both got something out of this.'

Her face in the dim light of the back of the car looked as if it was carved out of marble. 'I'll be the perfectly attentive wife, Rafael, don't worry.' And she jerked her chin out of his hand and looked away again.

In the interval of the performance Isobel went to the powder room—as much to escape Rafael for a few minutes as to repair her non-existent make-up. It was happening again. He was using the excuse of being in public and putting on a front to touch her at every opportunity and her nerves were shredding fast.

To her relief the powder room was empty, and she splashed some water on her face. She heard someone come in and only half looked up, but froze when she saw a stunningly beautiful woman looking straight at her. As she watched, she saw the woman lock the door behind her so no one else could come in.

Isobel didn't feel fear, she just felt bemused. She stood up and shook her hands out, wiped at her face with a towel.

'So how does it feel to know you've married the most elusive bachelor in Argentina?'

A foreboding chill crawled down Isobel's spine as she met the woman's dark slumberous eyes in the mirror. 'I'm sorry— do I know you?'

The woman came closer, to stand before the mirror, admiring her own reflection. Isobel moved back, but had to admit she was gorgeous. Long midnight-black hair, sultry feline features and a body that was poured seductively into a gold lamé dress. It was a bit too obvious for Isobel's tastes, but...

'I'm Rafael's ex-fiancée.' She turned around and held out a hand. 'Pleased to meet you.'

Isobel's throat went dry as she wondered for a sickening moment how she had not recognised her. And how had Rafael let a temptress like this walk away from him? She was everything Isobel wasn't, and Isobel was too stunned to castigate herself for thinking like that.

Isobel ignored her hand and sidled towards the door. The first bell rang for people to go back to their seats and she breathed a sigh of relief. 'I'd better get back. Rafael will be wondering where I am.'

The other woman crossed her arms and her eyes went to cat-like slits. 'So you got him in the end? You know, his arranged marriage to you was one of the things I used to show him how trapped he was.' The woman's full mouth went into a bitter line. 'But then I was greedy, and when he lost everything it was too much of a risk to stick around. How could I know he'd make it all back and then some?'

Isobel's brain throbbed. 'Lost everything...?' What was this woman talking about?

The woman laughed harshly and sent a scathing glance up and down. 'Look at you. You're not even wearing make-up. You could never have hoped to get Rafael without an arranged marriage. He's only ever felt passion for one woman—*me*. Why do you think he was about to elope with me?'

The warning bell rang again outside and, feeling overwhelmed, Isobel grabbed blindly for the lock on the door and turned it, all but falling out in a heap. She felt clammy. To her utter surprise Rafael was waiting on the other side.

He took her arm. 'I was just coming to look for you. Is something wrong? You look ill.'

Just then the door opened again, and the woman sauntered out. Unable not to watch, Isobel took in Rafael's reaction with sick fascination. His eyes narrowed and his face flushed. Clearly he was not immune to this woman. Isobel felt even more nauseous.

'Ana,' he bit out.

'Rafael, darling,' the woman purred. 'I wanted to come and introduce myself to your lovely new wife. After all, we almost had so much in common.'

Rafael's hand had tightened on Isobel's arm so much that she bit back a cry.

'Actually, Ana, you've got so little in common it's almost funny.'

And with that Rafael strode away, dragging Isobel in his wake. When she could finally speak she managed to get out, 'Rafael—my arm. You're hurting me.'

He finally stopped, and she wrenched her arm from his grasp, rubbing it. Now she was feeling mortified and angry. 'What on earth was *that* all about?'

He looked a little shell-shocked, and something curiously like hurt ripped through Isobel's chest.

He ran a hand through his hair with an impatient gesture and then said curtly, 'Nothing. I just haven't seen her in a long time. Come on, or we'll miss the second half.'

That night Isobel lay in bed and couldn't sleep. Her insides roiled and all she could keep thinking about was Rafael saying to his ex-fiancée, *'You've got so little in common it's almost funny.'*

Following their exchange before they'd gone out for the evening Isobel had fully expected Rafael to take her to his bed that night. But after bumping into Ana Perez he'd been abnormally quiet and subdued, barely bidding Isobel good-night when they'd returned to the house. And she knew why—what it had to be. Because seeing her next to Ana Perez had reminded him of everything he was missing from his marriage.

Passion and love.

No matter how cynical his exterior, he couldn't truly *not* want that.

It wasn't hard to remember the passionate pictures of them all those years before, when they'd been engaged. He'd looked devastated to see his ex-fiancée that evening. Isobel turned on her side and stared sightlessly into the gloom, unwilling to acknowledge how much that thought hurt.

Isobel felt hollow-eyed the next morning when she came down to breakfast. She'd deliberately come down later to try and avoid Rafael, but he was sitting there in shirt and tie, finishing his coffee when she came in. He glanced up and took her in.

'You look like hell.'

'Thanks,' she muttered, and sat down, feeling even more exposed.

Rafael cleared his throat. 'I'm sorry you were subjected to Ana's unique brand of social grace last night.'

Isobel affected blithe unconcern as she poured herself some coffee. 'Oh, *that*? I'd forgotten all about meeting *her*.'

'Yes,' he said tightly. 'Well, it won't happen again. I can assure you of that.'

Isobel flicked him a quick glance so she wouldn't have to look at him properly. 'Look, really, it's no big deal. You were engaged. It'd be weirder if she'd said nothing at all.'

Rafael went very still. 'Just exactly what *did* she say?'

Isobel squirmed in her seat and cursed herself silently, especially when Rafael said grimly, 'Isobel, I'm not leaving here until you tell me, and you can forget about pretending you talked about the weather. I know exactly what she's like.'

Isobel's insides felt as if they were being lacerated. His interest in what Ana had said had to be evidence that he still felt something for her, or else why the need to know?

So she blurted out, 'Fine. She wanted me to know that if you hadn't lost everything when you had, you'd be married to her by now.' Rafael snorted indelicately, and Isobel was reminded of her curiosity of the night before. 'What did she mean about losing everything?'

Rafael looked as grim as Isobel had ever seen him—face taut, the lines harsh. 'What my dear ex-fiancée was alluding to was the fact that our engagement had disastrous repercussions. My father died just after we announced the engagement, leaving the company in disarray. When rumours emerged that Ana and I might elope, and thus break the legal agreement between *our* families, investors and banks washed their hands of me, sure that I wouldn't be able to turn things around like my father always had.'

'Elope?' Isobel repeated faintly, recalling just then that Ana had mentioned it last night.

Rafael's eyes were cold and black. 'Ana thought it would be romantic. She played on the fact that I felt trapped by this agreement, that I was promised in marriage to someone who was barely a teenager at the time. She thought eloping would be the quickest way to entice me into marriage, but before we could get that far my finances collapsed overnight.'

Isobel shook her head, trying to absorb this information and ignore the way it made her feel to know that he'd been willing to elope for love. 'But what about your brother? Wasn't he—?'

'My brother had his own concerns by then, in Greece. It was up to me to get things back on track. And I did—before we could lose our home and before we could lose the *estancia*.' His mouth twisted bitterly. 'However, Ana didn't trust my ability. She ran, and within months she'd married a Swiss industrialist who could keep her in the manner to which she'd become accustomed.'

All Isobel could think of in that moment was how hollow and empty her belly felt. 'I had no idea…' she said ineffectually.

'Why would you?' He shrugged nonchalantly. 'The press had a field day, but once I started to make money again it was soon forgotten and I was welcomed back into the fold.'

Rafael stood then, and his chair sounded harsh on the floor. Isobel flinched slightly.

'Still flinching, Isobel?' His voice sounded unbearably harsh, as if talking about the past had tapped into something within him. She looked up.

Rafael leant down and put his finger under her chin, tipping her face up to his. For a terrified moment she was afraid he was going to kiss her, just when she was feeling far too vulnerable. But then he said, 'I'm bored with talk of the past and ex-fiancées. You are my wife now, Isobel, and I'm done with waiting. Tonight I'll have you in my bed. But first we have to entertain a business contact. Be ready to go out at eight.'

Still a little dazed and stunned at what had just transpired, Isobel finished her breakfast and went out to the hall. She saw that someone had put the post in the door and went to pick it up. Along with it was one of the tabloid papers that Juanita liked reading.

When Isobel flipped open the paper fully there was a lurid headline proclaiming that Ana Perez was back in town, and an old picture of Rafael and Ana just after they'd announced their engagement. They were hand in hand, with Rafael curving his other hand protectively around Ana's face to shield her from the paparazzi. Rafael looked so young, vibrant and handsome, with a softness to his face that she'd never seen.

Nausea surged again just as Juanita appeared. Isobel all but pushed the letters and the paper into her hands and fled, leaving Juanita to look at the paper curiously.

'I believe you're a professional dancer?'

Isobel turned to Rita, the wife of Rafael's business contact and smiled weakly, trying to ignore the fact that her head spun a little with the movement. 'Well, not professional. Although I did teach tango when I lived in Paris.'

The middle-aged woman sighed expressively. 'My husband and I went to a tango show last night. It's just about the most erotic and sexy thing I've ever seen. I'd love to be able to dance like that.'

Isobel flushed when she remembered how it had felt to

dance with Rafael in Paris and took another sip of her wine, knowing that she was playing with fire but needing something, anything, to block out the fact that here she was, all but colluding in her husband's business concerns, and that tonight Rafael expected her to—

'Go easy on that wine, Isobel. I don't want to have to carry you out of here.'

Rafael said it quietly, just to her and with a smile, but also with a clear warning in his eyes. It made Isobel rebelliously pick up her wine again and take an even bigger gulp this time.

He said urbanely to Rita, 'Isobel and I would love to perform a tango for you if the opportunity arises. When you're here for longer perhaps she could give you a few lessons.'

The woman stuttered. 'Oh—oh, no, I couldn't expect that—'

Isobel took pity on her and said effusively, 'Don't be silly. I'd love to teach you the basics. It'd be no problem at all. I have so much time on my hands these days I almost don't know what to do with myself.'

The woman looked from Rafael to Isobel, clearly registering the barbed comment, and just said, 'Well, that'd be great, honey. Thank you.'

Isobel took another drink, almost revelling now in Rafael's dark, censorious glances. Who did he think he was anyway? She knew the wine was going straight to her head, despite the dinner they'd eaten.

Bob, Rita's husband, who sat opposite, engaged her in conversation, but Isobel found herself having to carefully enunciate everything she said. In truth she wasn't able to keep track of much of the conversation around her, knowing that on some level she was blocking it out because she didn't want to hear just how ruthless Rafael was. It wasn't long before she began to feel a little sick and knew she'd gone too far. She wasn't even really aware any more of what she was saying.

Feeling a sudden urge to get some air, she moved to get up. A surge of dizziness made her sit straight back down. Immediately, Rafael's arm was around her. She heard him murmur something about 'getting home…long day…not long after honeymoon…' and then he was supporting her out of the restaurant.

In the back of the car on the way home, the alcohol provided a nice safe distance from the waves of anger she could feel coming off Rafael. She started to giggle when she imagined it like a force field, protecting her from his wrath.

His filthy look in her direction made her giggle even harder—and then she was gone, tears streaming down her face, nearly bent double over her knees, unable to catch her breath.

It was only when Rafael reached in to pluck her out of the car that she realised that they were home. Rafael lifted her into his arms, and instantly Isobel's giggles stopped and turned into hiccups. Her head spun ominously, but then cleared again.

His body felt taut and hard and his face was grim. Her hands went around his neck and the surprisingly silky strands of his hair brushed against her fingers. Instinctively, she moved them to feel more. She couldn't take her eyes off his mouth.

Everything coherent disappeared from Isobel's head. All she knew was that she was in Rafael's arms, and any concerns and inhibitions were dissolving like snow on hot coals at the feel of his body so close to hers. It was amazingly unclear to her now why she'd insisted on resisting him.

The front door was open and he shouldered his way through. She could feel his chest muscles contract and move against her. Isobel brought her hand round and pressed a finger against his mouth, a cord tightening in her belly. 'You've got the most beautiful mouth—do you know that?'

She was aware on some level that the words in her head weren't coming out as clearly as they should. They were flowing together in an incoherent slurred rush of words all joined up together.

Rafael twisted his head away and Isobel's hand fell to his neck. She started to pull at his bow tie to get to the buttons of his shirt. Frowning in concentration, she was barely aware of Rafael climbing the main stairs she was so intent on her task.

When the bow tie proved impenetrable to her clumsy ministrations she gave up with a huff and started to undo the other buttons of his shirt, sighing happily when she could slide a hand in and touch the warm skin of his chest. His heart was beating heavily against her hand and she felt unbearably hot all over. Waves of heat were coming and going, gathering intensity.

Swaying dangerously, she was hardly aware of Rafael standing her on her feet, or his curse. She looked up and his head was too far away. She wanted him to kiss her, *right now*, but wasn't even aware she'd articulated it with any success until he said caustically, 'Isobel, I am not taking my drunk wife to bed. When we make love you're going to be stone-cold sober and aware of every moment.'

She swayed again unsteadily, and then everything became a blur. All she knew was that she was lying down and Rafael's arms were around her. But then he was pulling back, taking them away.

'No!' she said impulsively, and caught him back. She ran her hands through his hair and pulled his head down, sighing voluptuously. 'Your hair feels like silk…kiss me, Rafael.'

She closed her eyes and pursed her lips, and heard Rafael say, 'I swear you'll be the death of me.'

She opened her eyes and tried to focus, but there were two Rafaels. 'So die a little…please…just kiss me.'

But Rafael was gone, and Isobel suddenly felt very strange as the whole room started to spin alarmingly.

When Isobel woke the next morning everything hurt. Especially her head and her stomach. She groaned and put a hand to her head, massaging it delicately. And with slow and devastating thoroughness everything trickled back. The dinner, Rita and Bob, the wine…Rafael carrying her up the stairs. Her begging him to kiss her…and then, worst of all, her hunched over the toilet as the entire contents of her wine-laden belly came up. It was still blurry, but she definitely remembered a presence with her, holding her and handing her a wet cloth, making her brush her teeth. *Rafael.*

She groaned even louder and buried her face in her pillow. How could she ever hope to beg for more space after her wanton theatrics last night? After a long moment she sat up carefully, only noticing then that she was in her bra and pants. With another groan she threw back the cover and went to stand up, but just then her door opened and Rafael stood on the threshold, tall and glorious and stern. Isobel scrambled for the sheet to cover herself.

'Do you mind?' Her voice felt unbearably rusty.

He arched an incredulous brow. 'Believe me, *querida*, you really don't have the right to act outraged when you tried to strip me last night. I barely got out of here with my dignity intact.'

Isobel tucked the sheet around her, face flaming. 'So I got a little merry…'

He came closer, and Isobel had to look up and her head hurt.

'*A little merry?* You were drunk, and after only two glasses of wine. I've never seen anything like it.'

'I told you I don't have a head for alcohol.'

'And yet you ignored me when I told you to go easy. You can get as drunk as you like at home, Isobel, but not out in public as my wife. I had to practically carry you out of that restaurant in front of an important business associate and his wife.'

She winced again, but not even hearing him mention his business contact could eclipse the nausea she already felt.

'And, much as I appreciate your crude effort at seduction, like I said last night, when we make love you're going to be stone-cold sober and you will remember every moment.' He started to back away and then stopped. 'I'm going to be working late tonight, but we've been invited to a polo tournament tomorrow. I hope that you'll be more in control of yourself by then.'

Isobel nodded curtly as waves of mortification threatened to drown her. Rafael just shook his head and gave her a look that said he was satisfied he'd brought his wife back into line, then strode out of the room. As soon as he was gone, Isobel collapsed back on the bed and looked at the ceiling.

An unsavoury thought occurred to her: had she subconsciously sabotaged last night not just out of disgust for his business ethics, or fear of her uncontrollable response to her husband, but because of the inevitable comparison Rafael would make between her, Isobel, and the sultry Ana Perez?

Isobel sat up. A novice like her could never match up to a practised seductress like Ana. Once Rafael had slept with her and found her wanting he'd realise what a mistake he'd made. There was no way a man as virile as him would want to tie himself to a wife he didn't want to sleep with…especially not after running into the love of his life.

With an awful sense of inevitability washing over her, and feeling somehow rudderless, Isobel got up wearily and had a hot shower. The truth was that thought didn't comfort her, and thinking about Rafael finding out what a let-down in bed she was was making her feel hollow inside.

Last night had given her a taste of the corporate life Rafael lived, and Isobel felt a surge of determination to take control of things herself. She wanted to prove that, whatever else happened, she was not going to be like her husband in business matters. She was in this situation and she had to make the best of things. What had Rafael said the other day? Something about the world being her oyster, and that she could do what she wanted…? Even as she thought of that, a kernel of an idea sprang to life in her head and, feeling enthusiastic for the first time in a long time, Isobel dried herself off and got dressed.

That evening, feeling tired but happy, Isobel waited in the lounge for Rafael to come home for dinner. Lots of property brochures were spread out before her. She heard a familiar heavy footfall and looked up to see Rafael filling the door frame. A shiver of foreboding slithered down her spine. He looked furious.

He strode into the room and threw down a paper onto the table in front of her. 'Want to tell me what the hell you've been up to?'

Isobel's mouth dropped open. She genuinely had no idea what Rafael was talking about. She looked down to see that the paper was an evening edition, and there on the front page was a grainy picture of her shaking a man's hand outside a decrepit building in La Boca, one of Buenos Aires's oldest districts. It must have been taken that morning.

There was a headline: *Does Romero know what his new wife is up to when he's not looking?*

Isobel looked up to see Rafael glowering, hands on hips. Bristling. She stood, too, because she felt so intimidated. 'I can explain, Rafael.'

'Please do. I'm just dying to know why you were doing deals with dubious-looking strangers in broad daylight. Don't tell me you have a drug habit you've been keeping a secret?'

Now Isobel bristled. Her hands clenched to fists at her sides. 'I thought you told me to occupy my time, Rafael—that I wasn't a prisoner and that I could do what I wanted with my newfound fortune?'

A muscle clenched in Rafael's jaw. 'You can. But not when you lose your security detail and wander into seedy areas.'

Isobel gasped. 'Since when do I have a security detail?'

Rafael slashed an impatient hand through the air. 'Of course you have a security detail. You're a target, Isobel, and today you've proved that you're a ridiculously easy one.'

Isobel was livid now. 'Well, if you'd informed me that I *was* a virtual prisoner then I might have been able to keep my gaolers informed as to my movements. If you recall I did try and phone you this morning to tell you what I was doing, but you refused to take my call.'

Rafael's anger abated for one second. Isobel *had* tried to call, but he'd been wrapped up in a series of intense meetings and even knowing that she'd called had distracted him unnecessarily. By the time he'd been free there had been a message from her to say it hadn't been important. And something weak had kept him from calling her anyway…

Stiffly, he said now, 'I'm sorry about that, but you rang at a busy time.'

Now Isobel waved a hand, the colour in her cheeks high, disgust making her gut clench. 'Yes, I can well imagine that you were extremely busy figuring out just how you and your nice American partner are going to get rid of the unsightly problem of hundreds of illegal immigrants in the complex you're negotiating to buy out.'

Rafael went ominously still. His voice dripped with ice. 'I see you've been following reports in the newspapers. You're a little out of date, though.'

Isobel flushed guiltily, and cursed herself for saying that. 'Whatever, Rafael. I know what your priorities are. Business first and convenient trophy wife second.' She stopped for a moment and struggled with her breath, trying to calm down. He'd never listen to her like this. She bit her lip, looking at the paper again and then at Rafael. 'I want to set up my own business venture.'

'What are you talking about?'

Isobel took a deep breath. 'I want to open up a dance studio. A tango dance studio. I know there's a million of them in Buenos Aires, but I want to teach children as well as adults. Offer all different kinds of dance classes in a non-exclusive way.'

Isobel could feel a little of her enthusiasm coming back. 'And I've also been thinking about dance therapy—for disadvantaged kids, or kids who have learning disabilities. A psychotherapist friend in Paris has been working with kids through dance and the results can be really amazing…' Isobel trailed off and looked at Rafael warily. He still hadn't spoken.

She gestured with a hand to the property brochures on the table. 'That's what I was doing today. I wanted to see what kind of places were for sale or rent…and I've always liked La Boca so I thought it might be a good place to start…'

Rafael just looked at Isobel for a long moment. He struggled against waves of affront and anger to know that she'd judged him so arbitrarily on the basis of a newspaper report. He hated that he cared that she thought so little of him.

She was still dressed in the plain jeans and long-sleeved T-shirt she'd been photographed in earlier. She looked all at once sexy as hell and vulnerable. And coming home to him now was the realisation that he still hadn't bedded his own wife. When his head of security had called him earlier to inform him that she'd gone out and they'd lost her, the rush of panic to his gut had been nothing short of cataclysmic.

The remembered panic and that lingering anger galvanised him now. 'I will not have my wife setting up a dance studio to teach tango on the streets alongside people who perform for a few pesos.'

Isobel gasped; her eyes flashed. 'It would *not* be on the streets alongside street performers, and you know it. I'm talking about setting up a proper studio, bringing money into a disadvantaged area and helping children and adults from all parts of society. Not just the rich kids. I'd also be offering job opportunities.'

Isobel watched as Rafael stepped back a pace and put his hands in his pockets.

'You will not embarrass me like this, Isobel—wandering around talking to anyone and everyone. Whether you like it or not, you are from a certain part of society, and you would do well to remember that you have a responsibility to me as well as yourself. Your image will be scrutinised by everyone in our social circle, your every movement analysed. And mine by proxy. I'm involved in a delicate business negotiation. I can't afford to have a loose cannon for a wife.'

Rafael heard the words coming out of his mouth and a part of him winced inwardly. He sounded like a pompous snob, but he couldn't stop himself. His inarticulate need to control Isobel was too strong. Her behaviour today had brought up far too many conflicting emotions for him to deal with. And he couldn't think straight when she was in front of him like this.

Tight-lipped with fury, Isobel bent down and swept all the property brochures off the table. She stalked over to a bin in the corner where she deposited the lot. She turned around, stiff-backed, and said curtly, 'I'm glad we got this sorted. Now I know exactly how small the cage is that I'm supposed to live in. From now on I'll be sure to be appropriately attired every day and remember my Ps and Qs and not to think for myself again. If you'll excuse me, I'm going to bed. I've lost my appetite.'

She walked out of the room and Rafael sat down on the sofa, arms resting on his knees. For the first time in his life he had to admit to feeling out of his depth. The photo in the paper caught his eye. Isobel was smiling warmly into the man's face. He hadn't seen her smile like that at *him* once…

She'd smiled at the *estancia*, but that had been after the exhilaration of riding in the great stretches of the pampas and hadn't been anything to do with him.

He flicked the pages over and saw another headline, which mocked him now. Clearly Isobel didn't care enough to investigate what Rafael was really up to. Her opinion was based on an erroneous newspaper report published weeks ago. He had to concede he hadn't exactly done anything to change that opinion, but he'd told himself that he would not let her opinion get to him, that he didn't care what she thought, because if he did it would mean that he'd learnt absolutely nothing about self-protection. That he was as potentially weak and vulnerable as he had been all those years before, when Ana Perez had nearly destroyed him.

One thing he had to admit made a curious form of dread trickle through him: when he'd believed himself in love with Ana, he'd never cared this much about her opinion of him. Wearily, he took the paper and put it in the bin, and then went to find Juanita to ask her if she'd take some food up to Isobel's room.

CHAPTER EIGHT

THE following day was a Saturday, and they were going to the polo tournament, and then later to a charity dinner, with Rafael's business associate Bob and his wife. Isobel was still feeling bruised and hurt by the evidence of how far Rafael was willing to go to control her. Her plan had been a bright glimmer of hope and he'd doused it.

Determined not to let him see how hurt she felt, she put her armour on. She wore a white designer trouser suit, stiletto heels and dark glasses. She was waiting for him at the front door and didn't turn around when she heard him behind her.

He strode past her and opened the passenger door of the four-wheel drive. Isobel walked over to get in, ignoring Rafael's helping hand. She thought she heard him sigh impatiently.

He strode around the front of the car, darkly handsome in a charcoal suit, white shirt and slim tie. Her heart clenched despite herself when she noticed that he looked tired, and she fought down the concern that came out of nowhere to grip her. What was wrong with her? she wailed inwardly. If anything, last night should have given her ample reason to hate Rafael. He'd been unbearably snobbish, priggish and controlling.

To have her worst suspicions of him confirmed like this made her feel unaccountably bleak inside, and Isobel didn't attempt to make conversation on the way to the polo ground. As soon as they got there, Rafael swept her along in his wake to the exclusive VIP area, where they were greeted by uniformed waiters carrying trays of champagne.

A little later Isobel was making polite conversation with Rita. She'd noticed how the woman had glanced nervously at Isobel's drink and Isobel had winced inwardly, still mortified to know she'd caused a scene of any kind.

The polo match went on in the background, but it was obvious from Rafael's intense conversation with Bob that this was just a backdrop for more negotiations. Rita chattered inanely about the shopping in Buenos Aires being so much better than in Texas, where they were from, and Isobel tried her best to look interested.

When Rita excused herself to go to the bathroom Isobel breathed a sigh of relief, wondering how much longer this torture was likely to last. She pulled distractedly at her jacket, realising that a tag must still be attached somewhere as something was scratching against her skin.

Just then Rafael's arm snaked around her waist and he drew her in to his side. He bent his head and said quietly, '*Stop* fidgeting.'

Isobel looked up, and heat flooded her belly when she saw the lazy smile on his mouth and the latent heat in his eyes. She couldn't believe it. Even now, after his behaviour last night, she *still* reacted to him. At the last second, before his charisma could suck her under, she reminded herself it was just because they were in public and he was putting on an act. She wished she was immune to it by now.

Rafael had been trying to keep his attention on his conversation but it was impossible with Isobel beside him. When he'd come down this morning to greet her she'd been at the breakfast table, pale-faced and impassive.

She'd flicked him a glance and said quickly, gesturing to her tracksuit, 'Don't worry—I'm not planning on wearing this to the polo tournament. I've been working out in the gym.'

'Isobel—' he'd started to say, but she'd cut him off.

'Really, Rafael, you don't have to say anything. I'm glad we know where we stand. I know my place and I'm firmly in it now. That's all you want from me, isn't it? How hard can it be?' She'd laughed, but it had sounded brittle. 'I mean, in a country where most of the population has to struggle just to make ends meet I've got nothing to complain about, have I?' She'd wiped her mouth with a napkin and stood up. 'I'll go and get ready.'

Her words came back to him, and his belly clenched again in self-disgust. He pulled her in even closer but could feel subtle resistance in her body. He didn't want her like this. Everything he'd said last night had been wrong. And, however vulnerable it made him feel now, he had to do whatever it took to bring back the Isobel he knew—the wife he knew he wanted.

Isobel was gritting her teeth not to respond to the way her body seemed to want to mould into Rafael's. His hand was making soothing circular motions against her waist and she fought not to let it affect her.

And then Rafael said to Bob, sending Isobel a quick, enigmatic glance, 'You may have seen pictures of my wife in the paper yesterday?'

Isobel tensed all over and her stomach plummeted. She saw Bob flush brick-red and mutter something incoherent, and realised then that Rafael had been right. The looks and whispers she'd thought she'd noticed on their arrival *had* been in large part because of the picture in the paper.

But now something much bigger was making her belly tighten with dread. She couldn't help but think that Rafael

meant to ridicule her, here in front of this man—tell him
about his wife's grand plan and send her up while protecting
his own reputation. She should have known that someone
like him would never have endorsed her plan.

She tried to pull away from him and the dread mounted.
He was opening his mouth to speak, and she hissed,
'Rafael...please don't do this.'

Tears prickled at the back of her eyes to think that she'd
not anticipated his cruelty.

But then he started speaking. 'I'm very proud to say that
Isobel has decided to open up a dance studio in La Boca. It's
always been known locally as a bit of a no-go area, so I think
she's made a strategic and generous decision in choosing to
open up there.'

Shock rippled through Isobel. She wondered for a second
if she'd misheard and looked up questioningly. Bob, whose
face had flushed so tellingly when he'd all but admitted to
reading a piece of tabloid fluff, now said jovially, 'Two
bleeding hearts in one marriage? Rafael, you'd better watch
that reputation of yours. If you weren't such an astute businessman you'd be in serious danger of becoming the pin-up
boy of liberals everywhere! Especially now that your wife is
clearly cut of the same cloth.'

Isobel's gaze swung back to her husband. She could feel
the tension come into his body, saw him grimace and then
quirk a small smile. 'This isn't the time or place for that conversation, Bob. We'll discuss it later.'

Bob turned to Isobel. 'Have you found a property you like
yet?'

Rita had returned, picked up the conversation, and was
joining in enthusiastically, rhapsodising again about the tango
show they'd seen.

Rafael cut in. 'Isobel's plans are a little more far-reaching than just a standard dance studio…' He looked down at her indulgently, for all the world the doting husband. 'Why don't you tell them what you want to do?'

Dumbfounded, and dying to know what Rafael had cut Bob off from talking about, she found it hard to take her eyes away from Rafael, still wondering was going on. Hesitantly, she started to tell the others of her plans, half expecting to hear Rafael burst out laughing and ridicule her. But when he didn't, she found herself becoming more enthusiastic, until she'd almost forgotten Rafael's initial reaction.

It was only later, when they were in the car and driving home, that Isobel realised the day had passed quickly after that, and had been surprisingly enjoyable. She turned to face Rafael. 'Are you going to tell me what that was all about?'

He flashed her a look and his jaw tightened. 'I owe you an apology. I completely overreacted last night. I think your idea does have merit, and normally I'd be one of the first people to encourage bringing growth and investment into an area like La Boca.'

Isobel saw his hands tighten on the steering wheel.

'When I heard that the security men had lost you and then that photograph surfaced…I just saw red.'

'I did try to tell you…' Isobel pointed out quietly, stunned to hear Rafael saying this.

His mouth quirked. 'I know. I've learnt my lesson. I won't miss one of your calls again.'

Isobel sat back and felt a very ominous fluttering in her chest. 'Thank you for your support today.'

He cast her another quick look as they pulled into the forecourt of the house. 'I'll take some time off work on Monday and come with you to see some properties.'

Isobel blustered, not sure why that idea was so threatening. 'No, you don't have to. You're far too busy.'

Rafael smiled wryly. 'How much did that man in the photograph quote you for the building you'd just viewed?'

Isobel named a figure, and Rafael winced and shook his head. 'He saw you coming a mile away. He probably knew exactly who you were, too, which would have tripled his quote. No, I'm coming with you next time. Let him try and do a deal with *me*.'

They were walking through the front door when Isobel couldn't keep it back any more. 'What was Bob talking about earlier, when he called you a bleeding heart liberal?'

Rafael turned around slowly. Isobel could see his face tighten up, his expression shutter. 'He was referring to a headline in the paper.'

'What paper?' Isobel asked now, getting impatient with Rafael's obvious reluctance to explain himself.

His jaw tightened. 'The same paper you yourself appeared in. Just a few pages on.'

Isobel waited, but clearly Rafael wasn't about to enlighten her, so with an impatient sigh she went into the lounge and to her relief saw that the paper was still in the bin. She pulled it out and flicked through the pages until her eye caught on a headline with an article below.

> Rafael Romero and his bleeding heart try to do a deal
> to encourage hundreds of skilled illegal immigrants to
> come home by buying out a failed electronics plant…

She scanned the piece quickly, feeling her insides constrict more and more as she did so. Bob Caruthers was Rafael's US partner in negotiations for reopening the plant in

Argentina with the same workers who'd originally gone to the
US seeking work. Anyone who wanted to stay on in the States
was going to be offered free legal aid to obtain legitimate work
visas, and Rafael was taking personal responsibility for every
one of the immigrants.

The paper dropped out of Isobel's hands. She felt sick, but
this time for entirely different reasons. She felt shamed. She
could hardly meet Rafael's eyes. She'd been labouring under
a very erroneous misapprehension over Rafael's work ethics
from the very first moment she'd met him.

He looked as defiant as she felt humbled, and somewhere
she recognised that he hated this—being in this position.

'I'm sorry, Rafael. I had no right to judge what you do on
the basis of the one report I read.'

His mouth twisted. 'I can't entirely blame you. We needed
to keep it quiet for as long as possible to ensure the protection of the immigrants. I'm involved in a programme with the
government to try and create jobs here, to dissuade our young
skilled workers from leaving. Bob Caruthers is based in the
US; it's Bob I have to deal with over the demise and rebuild-
ing of the company. It's been a delicate negotiation so far, and
Bob still hasn't signed the last contract to seal the deal. He's
under no obligation to sanction the move of operations to
here.'

Isobel just looked at Rafael, and felt the earth shift and
sway under her feet.

Rafael's chest felt tight with the way Isobel was looking
at him. Her gaze was so…penetrating, and full of some indefinable emotion. Something was rising within him and he
knew only one way to avoid looking at what that was.

In three long strides he'd crossed the room and cupped
Isobel's face in his hands. He felt her startled breath against

his palms and his body tightened with need. Her eyes were huge and intensely dark. She opened her mouth, and the desire rushing through Rafael's blood made him say, more curtly than he'd intended, '*No*. I don't want to hear it. Enough. Tonight you'll be in my bed, Isobel.'

A short while later, changed for the charity function, Isobel had herself rigidly in control. She was aware of Rafael flicking her glances in the back seat of the car, and each one fell like a hot caress on her bared and too sensitive skin.

She wore a strapless cocktail dress, fitted to the knee, and her legs were primly together, slanted to the side, as far away from Rafael as possible. She was still reeling from the revelation of finding out exactly what Rafael had been working on and how wrong she'd been. It made her feel now as if a layer of protective skin had been ripped away, leaving her exposed and vulnerable. Too exposed and vulnerable to face the prospect of sleeping with Rafael that night.

She cast him a quick, surreptitious glance. He was looking ahead, coolly remote, and Isobel shivered. She couldn't hide any longer.

After a short journey they pulled up outside one of Buenos Aires's oldest and grandest hotels. Isobel's door was opened by a liveried doorman and she stepped out to be greeted by Rafael taking her hand in a firm grip. Quashing the urge to pull away, she gritted her teeth against the sensations shooting up her arm and let him lead her into the thronged and glittering function room.

Hundreds of dinner tables were set around a dance floor, which was currently occupied by tables showing off the lots for the charity auction. After dinner, when the lots had been auctioned off—Rafael having spent a ludicrous amount of money—the staff started clearing the dance floor.

Despite herself, Isobel's distaste for this superficial social scene rose up again. Rafael leant close, and it took all her restraint not to move back. His evocative scent was teasing her nostrils mercilessly.

'What is wrong with you? You look like you've swallowed a lemon.'

Isobel tightened her jaw. 'I just find it hard to sit here and watch the elite throwing their money around when the charity in question probably gets a bare percentage just for the privilege of having its name mentioned in such exalted circles.'

Rafael's voice was deep and close, lightly mocking. 'You're too quick to judge again.'

Isobel burned at being reminded of how quick and absolute her judgment had been.

'It's all a game, just like everything else. The people you see here are the most powerful in the country. To a large extent you're right in your assessment. But you're discounting what goes on in tandem with this—for instance, the fact that I've donated a disgustingly large amount of money to a cancer charity chaired by the Marquesa Consuela Valderosa, who is holding court on the table over there, means that she will now feel compelled, in the nicest possible way, of course, to lend her illustrious name and support to a much less monied charity of my own choice. It's all about getting what you want from people. You just have to know how to play the game, Isobel.'

Isobel looked at him speechlessly. His eyes were dark and hypnotic, and she had the strong suspicion he was talking about the games he had accused her of playing with him. She felt hot inside.

Just then Rita leant across the table and said excitedly to

Isobel and Rafael, 'They're playing that tango music from *Scent of a Woman*. Would you two dance for us…please?'

Isobel looked at Rafael helplessly, her belly quivering as she remembered how he'd strode across the room earlier and taken her face in his hands. He hadn't even kissed her, but when he'd turned and walked away she'd been trembling all over. She turned to Rita and started to say, 'I'm sorry— I don't know if—'

But Isobel felt her hand being taken and then she was being urged up to meet Rafael, who was looking down at her with a glint in his eye. 'Of course we'd love to dance a tango— wouldn't we, *carino*.'

Isobel hissed at Rafael as he led her to the dance floor, where a few couples were trying unsuccessfully to emulate the famous movie scene. 'My dress is too tight. I won't be able to dance properly.'

Rafael swept a look down and bent. All Isobel heard was a faint ripping sound. When he led her forward again she gasped as she felt a breeze, and looked down to see that Rafael had effortlessly ripped her dress to mid-thigh.

He brought her to the middle of the dance floor and she looked up at him, 'What on earth do you think—?'

But her words were cut off as Rafael expertly pulled her into his arms in a quick staccato move, forcing her weight forward and into him. His embrace was close and tight, their chests all but welded together as he started to move.

Isobel's feet followed naturally and instinctively, but this tango was not like the first time they'd danced in Paris. There was a simmering sensuality about this one, and it was worlds away from the kind of tangos their grandparents would have danced.

Isobel could feel the rip in her dress give way even more

as Rafael led her in a dizzying series of steps. She had to close her eyes when she saw that other dancers were stepping back to give them space and watch.

Isobel felt the slide of Rafael's leg between hers, forcing her leg up into the high kick known as a bolero. Her heart-rate was out of control. Then he displaced her weight and she had to lean into him even more.

When he twisted, so that she had to hook her leg under his, she could feel the tension in his powerful thigh muscle against the back of her leg. Her eyes opened with a mute plea for him to stop this sensual torture. His dark gaze glittered down at her, green and golden flecks standing out, making her throat dry. His intent was written all over his face: tonight he was going to make her his.

For a heart-stopping moment Isobel thought he was going to kiss her, and an instant fine layer of sweat seemed to spring up over her skin, but then Rafael broke the intense eye contact and kept dancing, pulling Isobel close again. She felt utterly exposed; this tango had become a display of Rafael's sensual domination over her, and with every move it felt as if he knew more and more just how badly she hungered for him. Along with everyone else watching.

Her fear of intimacy with this man, and what it might reveal to him and worse to *her* about her feelings for him, was hanging by a mere thread.

Finally the last chords of the achingly melancholic music died away. Isobel was breathing so hard she felt faint. She was in the classic supplicant tango pose, bent back and looking up into Rafael's face. People were starting to clap, but it was the triumphant look in his eyes that did it. Isobel acted completely on instinct. She ripped her hand from his and slapped him across his face.

Instantly silence fell. The clapping stopped. Isobel stood up awkwardly and attempted to walk off the floor, aghast at her reaction and what she'd done, but her wrist was caught and she was effectively twirled back into Rafael's hard body.

Before she could react everything disappeared as his mouth crashed down on hers, and the entire world seemed to explode inside her head. His mouth was hard and hot, the slide of his tongue too erotically seductive for her to fight. Angrily she matched him, aggressively stroking his tongue with hers, teeth nipping and biting at his lower lip. In that moment she truly hated him for reducing her to this tumult of feelings.

Her whole body was arched into his, as if she wanted to fuse with him there and then. It felt as if she was finally boiling over to a place of no return, all restraint washed away in an overwhelming tide of need. And then Rafael pulled away and stepped back, still holding Isobel's hand. Stunned, exposed, and very shaken, Isobel could only follow on wobbly legs as they walked off the dance floor. To her abject relief, other people had started to dance again.

Isobel was aware of Rafael issuing a curt instruction to someone and then they were out in the lobby, emerging into the cool night where his car was already waiting. In the back of the car, Isobel was still feeling crazily out of control.

She blurted out heatedly, 'I'm not going to apologise for that. It could have been a perfectly normal dance but you… you turned it into something positively indecent.'

Isobel shot him a glance to see his face stark. He ran a hand through his hair. She felt waves of tension crackle off him.

'The only thing indecent about that dance was the intensity of sexual frustration. I was no more capable of keeping that dance clean than you were of not twining your seductive body around mine like a purring cat.'

Isobel flushed as she recalled how it had been to feel the slide of his thigh between her legs. The cliché of the tango being a vertical expression of a horizontal act really wasn't such a cliché. The truth was, the dance had been exhilarating.

But right now one of her hands was holding the ripped sides of her dress together, in a futile attempt at some sort of modesty, and it felt as if she'd just been made love to in front of an entire audience.

'Need I remind you,' she said now, desperately trying to claw back some dignity, 'that you were the one who ripped my dress like some kind of caveman.'

They were at the house. Rafael said nothing and got out. Before Isobel could scramble out herself, Rafael was there. With a squeal Isobel saw Rafael duck low, and then she was out of the car and over his shoulder in a fireman's lift. She clamped her mouth shut, knowing that it would be futile to say a word, and the sensation of Rafael's powerful shoulder under her body was rendering her speechless anyway.

He climbed the stairs with ruthless intent in every step, and then walked all the way to his bedroom door, opened it and stepped inside, and then kicked it shut with a foot.

Suddenly Isobel was back on her feet and breathing harshly. A wild excitement mixed with fear sang in her blood. She knew she was powerless now, in the face of this overwhelming desire. She had no defences left. Rafael had chipped and picked away at them remorselessly.

It made her blurt out unthinkingly, 'Don't come near me. You're a Neanderthal.'

Tension and coiled energy bounced off Rafael in angry waves. A muscle twitched in his jaw. His eyes were black. Mere feet separated them, but Isobel fancied in that moment that she could feel his heart beating, thundering like hers.

She wanted him to close the distance, haul her into his arms and silence the cacophony of voices in her head and in her heart.

But then, as if a switch had been flicked, the tension disappeared. Rafael stepped back to the door. Isobel felt her body move slightly, as if they were joined by an invisible thread.

Rafael's face was carved from stone. Unreadable and harsh. And then, in a low blistering voice, he said, 'Damn you, Isobel.' And turned and walked out through the door.

CHAPTER NINE

THE minute he'd gone Isobel physically sagged, as if some life force had been stripped from her. She staggered back and sat heavily onto his bed. *What had just happened?* Every step of the way Rafael had met her head-on, time and time again. And suddenly…he hadn't. He'd walked away. Proving once again that his control was far greater than hers. Her body felt tight and aching with burning need.

When he'd put her down and she'd stepped away from him jerkily something had flashed across his face. Something that had looked tortured. Isobel recognised it now, because it was exactly how she felt. How she'd been feeling for a long time, although she'd been denying it to herself. Pushing it away, hiding from herself in the worst possible way.

She winced now when she thought of how carelessly she'd hurled those words at him, the way he'd flinched minutely and then shut down.

A compulsion rose and gathered force deep within her; there was only one thing to do, one place she wanted to be, one person she wanted to be with. There had only been one person since Rafael had kissed her on her eighteenth birthday.

A deeply feminine part of her wanted to make her mark on this man and she couldn't deny it any more. That was what it came down to. And she didn't have time to think about the ramifications or her precious integrity.

Rafael stood looking down into the dying embers of the fire Juanita must have lit earlier. He took a deep sip from the drink he'd just poured himself with a shaking hand. *A shaking hand.*

He grimaced, his head was in a tangled knot and his body burning thanks to that temptress upstairs. He tried to articulate to himself why he'd let her get to him *again.* Why hadn't he just tipped her back onto his bed? Right now he could be slaking his lust in a very satisfactory way. Exorcising this gnawing need in his body.

It was because he wanted Isobel so badly that he couldn't think straight. He'd realised in that moment upstairs that he'd never wanted a woman as badly as he wanted her. Not even Ana, and he'd thought he loved her. And when he thought about the implications of that—

He heard a sound come from the door and tensed.

Isobel pushed the door to the main reception room open to see the tall figure of Rafael standing in front of the fire. She saw him lift his hand and take a drink. And then he said harshly, 'Go away, Isobel. I'm not in the mood for any more of your games.'

Isobel flinched, and her heart ached in a very peculiar way. She came in and shut the door behind her, her pulse flowing thick and heavy through her veins as she took in the sheer breadth and power of Rafael's body in the black tuxedo. There was something curiously vulnerable about his stance.

He still didn't turn around, but seemed to have eyes in the back of his head when he said, 'I thought I told you—'

'I heard you.' Isobel cut him off softly. 'But I'm not leaving.' This was a pivotal moment. She knew it, and trembled all over with the knowledge of it. The truth was she didn't have the strength required to deny her attraction any more. She didn't have the strength to worry about what would happen if she allowed herself to be intimate with him. Her need for him was too great.

Rafael tipped back his head, drained whatever was in his glass and placed it too carefully on the mantelpiece. Slowly he turned around.

All Isobel could see was those dark eyes across the room, boring into her, through her. Burning her. He'd ripped open his bow tie and it dangled from his neck; the top buttons of his shirt were undone. Her breath constricted in her throat.

Rafael crossed his arms across his formidable chest. 'Come to hurl more insults, Isobel? Play the tease again?'

Isobel moved forward, but it felt as if she was wading through treacle. She stopped a few feet away from Rafael, her heart racing even harder. Her skin felt hot and tight, stretched across her bones. Her shoulders felt stiff.

'I...'

'I...*what*?' Rafael all but sneered, and moved as if to turn away again.

Instinctively, Isobel moved, too, and reached out, catching his jacket, feeling the strength of his arm through the material.

He stilled and she stopped dead.

'I...I'm sorry.'

Silence throbbed between them. He wasn't going to make this easy for her. Isobel knew that now. She let her hand drop but felt a fledgling sense of encouragement when he didn't turn away again.

Isobel bit her lip and then said in a rush, 'I never meant to be any kind of tease. I shouldn't have said...what I just said. I've been fighting you...fighting myself...and I can't any more.' She looked up at him, into his deep, unfathomable eyes, and spoke from the deepest part of her. 'I want you, Rafael…'

A harsh mocking smile touched Rafael's mouth, sending splinters into Isobel's heart.

'You *want* me?'

She nodded.

'I think I need you to clarify that statement, Isobel. We wouldn't want any confusion, would we? I don't like being called a Neanderthal, or being reduced to such *caveman* responses. Perhaps it's easier for you to sleep with a bleeding heart liberal than the corporate shark you believed me to be?'

Isobel winced again and looked down, unable to take the censure in his eyes even though she knew she deserved it. She looked up again and had the feeling that this moment was going to be a test of everything she was, everything she held dear.

All her preconceived notions had changed so much; the fact was that even if Rafael hadn't proved himself to be a man of integrity she knew she would still be standing here right now. The world she'd so dreaded coming back to had become something else entirely.

'I want you to make love to me, Rafael.' She swallowed painfully. 'I just…wasn't ready before. I couldn't—'

Rafael jerked a hand out of his pocket and slashed it through the air, cutting her off. 'Enough with the stuttering explanation, Isobel. It's cute, but unnecessary. You're here to tell me that you're ready to go to bed with me—is that it?'

Isobel blanched at his words, but nodded slowly.

A long moment stretched, and then Rafael casually took off his jacket and threw it on the arm of a nearby chair before going over and sitting down. Isobel turned and watched him warily.

With his elbows on the armrests, his face cast into dark

shadow, he looked at her and said throatily, 'Take off your clothes.'

Isobel just looked back at him, cold horror trickling through her. 'You want me to take my clothes off…here?'

Rafael inclined his head, barely leashed patience reaching out to envelop her. He drawled, 'It's not a riddle, Isobel.'

Isobel stalled again, knowing in every fibre of her body that she'd pushed him too far tonight and this was the consequence of her actions. She knew she couldn't leave now. To do so would cause irreparable damage. There was a delicate thread of trust here, and it wouldn't take much to break it. Even so, she asked huskily, unaware of the vulnerable quality in her voice, 'You want to make love here?'

Rafael was clearly not going to indulge her for long. He bit out, 'Believe me, Isobel, either you take your clothes off now, or I'll take them off for you—and I can't guarantee that they'll survive without being ripped again.'

Amidst the stomach-churning nerves and humiliation, Isobel felt a violent frisson of thrill and need rush through her. She concentrated on that, clinging to it like an anchor in the midst of a storm of self-recrimination at how utterly exposed she'd let herself become.

Rafael sat back like an ancient king, surveying his concubine, lean and powerful in the chair. With heat flaring in her belly, Isobel reached for the zip at the side of her dress, under her arm. Finding it, she started to pull it down, her fingers grazing her too sensitive skin, making goosebumps pop up.

All of a sudden she couldn't bear his cool regard and turned around. For a second tears pricked her eyes. She'd never in a million years imagined her first time would be like this—but then everything she'd expected and wanted had morphed out of all existence since she'd met this man.

The zip on her dress gave way with a sound that was unbearably loud in the quiet room, with only the dying crackles of the embers of the fire. With a deep breath Isobel let the dress fall to her waist, baring her back to Rafael.

Taking another deep breath, the tears prickling ominously and making her throat clog, Isobel pulled at the dress until it gave way, and let it drop to the floor at her bare feet. Closing her eyes for a long moment, feeling completely naked in just a slight pair of panties, she crossed her arms over her breasts and turned around.

Rafael was like a stone statue. Not moving a muscle. Just his eyes moved, all the way up from her feet…

Isobel's skin prickled as she stood there.

'Take your arms down. I want to see all of you.'

Biting her lip so hard that she tasted blood, Isobel finally let her arms drop, clenching her hands into fists. She had to consciously block out the poisonous thought that he would be comparing her to his more voluptuous ex-fiancée.

Where Rafael's gaze rested on her breasts, which felt inadequately small, she felt as though he'd touched her with a physical caress. The tips grew tight and she could feel them puckering, growing hard, aching for his touch, for his mouth. She wanted him so badly it was a physical pain, but he was intent on humiliating her.

Suddenly she knew she couldn't do this. Not standing before him like this, like some slave girl being bought. And not with the vivid memory of his stunning ex-fiancée so recent. Knowing that he'd loved her so passionately. With a strangled cry Isobel covered her breasts and said brokenly, 'I can't do this…like this. I'm sorry, Rafael.'

She turned around again, dropped her head. Tears were burning her eyes in earnest now.

Suddenly she felt movement behind her. Rafael had taken her arm to pull her back to face him. She felt a finger come to her chin, forcing her head up, and Rafael's voice was unbearably harsh. 'Isobel, I swear to God, you go too far this time—'

Then he stopped, and Isobel realised that he must have seen a tear escape.

'Open your eyes,' he said.

She shook her head, bit her lip again. And then Rafael undid her completely by cupping her jaw with his hands and smoothing his thumbs across her cheeks, wiping away the tears. She opened her eyes and looked up through a blur, arms still tight around her chest.

'I've never done this before, Rafael… I'm sorry that I can't be more sophisticated, but I…' a shuddering sigh came out '…I don't know how to seduce you.'

Rafael went very still. 'What are you saying?'

Her tears were clearing. She could see his face now, that beautiful sensual mouth. Heat was building again. His body was so close to hers.

'I've never slept with anyone.'

Rafael frowned, and then he uttered something that sounded like a curse. He must have seen something on her face because he suddenly said, '*No*, not you. I'm not angry with you. I thought…I suspected you might be innocent…but then when you said you'd had lovers…'

Isobel shook her head. 'I was angry. I didn't want you to know I was a virgin.'

Rafael snaked a hand around the back of her head, cradling it, and drew her in closer to his body. 'You're not saying you don't want to do this?'

Isobel shook her head again. 'I do…but not when you're being so cold.'

His eyes burnt her. He looked very serious all of a sudden, and Isobel's heart stuttered.

'Forgive me, Isobel.' He grimaced, his voice gruff. 'I was angry, and I want you so much… I didn't stop to think. Perhaps we could find somewhere a little more comfortable for your first time.'

Isobel's heart felt as if it was falling into a deep dark pit with no bottom. No going back now. 'Okay.'

With a smooth move Rafael wrapped his tuxedo jacket around her and lifted her into his arms. Within what felt like seconds, Rafael had ascended the stairs and they were back in his bedroom, with the door firmly shut.

She felt as if she'd been surrounding herself with walls and now they were all tumbling down. For a long moment Rafael looked at her, still holding her in his arms. His hand rested just below the curve of Isobel's bared breast. It hurt to breathe.

And then, as if loath even to let her down, he lowered his head and his mouth touched hers. His arms tightened around her. Isobel's arms came around his neck and she sank into the kiss, flames of passion escalating as the kiss grew hotter and heavier in seconds.

She shifted in his arms. Rafael's mouth moved over hers hungrily, and then he pulled away, so that he could press kisses along her jaw and, when her head fell back, down the delicate line of her neck. He pressed a kiss to the upper slopes of her breasts, and Isobel squirmed in his arms when a shaft of hot arousal went straight through her.

Slowly Rafael lowered Isobel down until she was standing. Her hands were still around his neck and she took them down hurriedly, embarrassed to be clinging to him like some kind of limpet. Her whole body felt like a fizzing ball of sensation and frustrated energy, and she watched impatiently as

Rafael drew off his bow tie and started to open his shirt. He took a step forward as he undid his shirt and Isobel walked back, his jacket falling from her shoulders. They moved like that all the way till the back of her knees hit his bed.

She sank down with a whoosh. Rafael tore off his shirt and her eyes went wide at the sight of his perfectly muscled torso, covered in a smattering of dark hair. Ridges of muscle led down to his lean waist, along with a line of hair which disappeared beneath where Rafael's hands were undoing his belt buckle.

Isobel swallowed and looked up again, her eyes caught by Rafael's. She heard the whisper of his zip being drawn down, his trousers dropping, and then, his eyes never leaving hers, he came and nudged her back onto the bed, coming to lean over her.

Rafael rested on his hands over her. He looked down her body and his gaze stopped on her uptilted breasts, their tips tingling. He brought up a hand and lightly brushed the back of his hand over one tight nipple, making Isobel bite her bottom lip to keep a mewl of exquisite agony from erupting.

Rafael looked at her again and said roughly, 'Do you know how long I've dreamt of this?'

She shook her head dumbly.

'Too long.'

And with that his mouth covered hers again, and Isobel was lost, drowning in a sea of more pleasure than she could ever have imagined existed. All fears and concerns of inadequacy were lost and forgotten. Isobel had no cognisance of anything other than trying to keep breathing.

Especially when Rafael's head moved down her body, and when his mouth hovered for a tantalising moment over her breast before his tongue teased and licked her nipple. Nearly crying with frustration, her back arching in silent demand,

Isobel couldn't help crying out when he finally sucked that tight peak into his mouth, her hands fisted in his hair.

Somehow Isobel realised that he'd manoeuvred them so that she was no longer hanging off the bed but on it properly. She felt his big body come between her legs, and that secret juncture spasmed in response. He pulled back and looked down, eyes glittering fiercely as he pulled her panties down and off her legs completely, dropping them somewhere out of sight.

She was utterly naked, but a quick look told her that Rafael still had his briefs on. Too overwhelmed to say anything she sank her head back and watched as he seemed to retreat, his hands moving down the sides of her body, following the line of her hips and thighs, before ascending again.

'Rafael...what are you...?' Her voice dried up when she felt him push her legs farther apart. He bent and pressed kisses against her belly and down farther. She tensed and could feel a light sweat break through her skin.

His hands came under her to cup her buttocks, and then she could feel his breath feather between her legs— Her head came up and she saw Rafael's face, flushed in the dim light.

'Relax, *querida*...you'll like it. I promise.'

Like what? And then Isobel's world stopped turning completely as Rafael's head bent and she felt his mouth and tongue on that wet and secret part of her. Her hands gripped the sheet. Her back arched.

'Raf...' his tongue speared her intimately '...ael...' She let out a gasp.

He was ruthless, remorseless, wringing a response out of her that she hadn't even known she had. His mouth was wicked, pushing her further and further from herself and everything she knew. She tried to hold on but in the end... couldn't. She felt herself arching almost off the bed, tensing all over, and then, after a stunning plateau of exquisite pleasure, she fell throbbing, down into Rafael's arms.

The earth was spinning. Isobel was dazed. She was vaguely aware of Rafael tugging his briefs off and then he was back, arms around her, looking down into her flushed face.

'Are you okay?' He smoothed a hand across one cheek and all Isobel could do was nod, even as her body clenched minutely. She could feel his hard erection against her thigh and instinctively reached a hand down to touch him.

Something inside her exulted when she wrapped her fingers around his turgid length, even as her mind balked a little at the blatantly masculine evidence of his size.

He hissed on an indrawn breath and he brought his hand down to cover hers, taking it away gently. 'We'll have plenty of time to explore at a more leisurely pace, *querida*…but right now I cannot wait.'

Instinctively, as Rafael moved over her, Isobel opened her legs. She felt him push against her, where a curiously unsatisfied ache was building. She shifted restlessly, and then Rafael was sliding into her, so slowly and carefully that she could see beads of sweat on his brow.

Isobel moved to meet him, but Rafael drew back and growled. '*No*. This is going to hurt a little. Let me dictate the pace…' He kissed her on the lips, still holding back, and said with a tortured-sounding laugh, 'Even now you have to meet me full-on…'

'Rafael,' Isobel groaned, feeling that elusive peak beckoning again. '*Please.* I'm fine.'

With his next move he thrust into her fully, and Isobel gasped when she could feel every hard inch of him embedded inside her. Her mouth made an O as she looked up, but with a slight movement of her hips she told Rafael she *was* fine.

Ever so slowly he withdrew, before thrusting in again, and that elusive peak came closer and closer to Isobel, teasing her with every thrust that Rafael made, faster now. She wrapped a leg around his back and groaned as she felt him slide even deeper within her.

As if he couldn't help himself his movements became more urgent. He thrust harder, deeper. Isobel's arms were wrapped around him, her chest arched up into his. She could feel her nipples scrape along the tautly muscled wall of his chest.

Their breaths grew ragged, hearts nearly bursting out of their chests, and whatever Isobel had experienced before was eclipsed by a blinding flash of sensation so acutely pleasurable that she tensed all over. Rafael drove in and out, and Isobel was unbearably sensitised for a moment, before she came crashing down again. She could feel the ripples of her orgasm clenching and unclenching around Rafael as he, too, tensed for a long, tortured moment until she felt his warm release deep inside her.

Shattered, all Isobel could do was lie there, with Rafael's deliciously heavy weight pinning her to the bed. After a couple of minutes she became aware of sweat-slicked skin, a musky smell, and damp hair clinging to her neck. A chill on her skin made her shiver slightly and Rafael moved, rolling off her, taking her with him, so that she lay sprawled over his chest, her body seemingly welded to his much harder one.

She felt a deep chuckle move his chest, and lifted her heavy head to look at him suspiciously. He just arched a brow, which spoke a multitude, and she ducked her head again, her face flaming.

This time when he moved he lifted the covers and rolled them both underneath, tucking Isobel close to his side. Rafael felt as though every one of his inner cells had shifted and regrouped into a new formation. Isobel was close against him, every inch of her lithe, graceful body touching his, and just thinking of that was making him harden all over again. He stifled a groan.

He felt her lift her head and ask, in a small, hesitant voice which sounded endearingly unlike her, 'Is it…always like that?'

Sheer masculine pride puffed up Rafael's chest, and a deep thrill ran through him to know that he'd been her first lover. He turned his head and pressed a kiss to where short tendrils of silky hair still clung damply to her forehead. 'For us…yes.'

He thought he felt her lips smile against his shoulder, but almost instantaneously he felt her body grow heavy and slack and her breathing grow deep and even.

He couldn't sleep. He felt as though his arms would have to be unwelded from where they held Isobel tight against him. He'd never felt like this before after making love with a woman. A face popped into his head and he all but sneered at the implication. Certainly never with *her*.

He shifted slightly so he could look down. All he could see was the smooth curve of Isobel's cheek and those plumped, swollen lips. Her cheeks were still flushed. A dart of recrimination struck him; he'd never meant to rip her dress like that in the hotel, but something in her wide eyes as she'd looked at him with such innocent provocation had said, *Look, don't touch.* And it had driven him over the edge of his endurance.

It was why he'd been so boorish earlier. He'd all but forgotten that he'd ever suspected her of being a virgin, too caught up in believing that she was experienced, teasing him, stringing him along, pushing him to his limits. When she'd covered her breasts with her arms downstairs he'd missed the tellingly vulnerable move, certain she was doing it again, and then he'd seen her tears… He could still feel the pain that had ripped through his chest.

His head fell back. All along she'd been innocent. And now she was tamed. His spitting hissing kitten with sharp claws was tamed at last. Rafael finally fell into a deep sleep with a smile on his face.

Isobel woke with a start, to find herself in an unfamiliar bed, with strange sensations running through a curiously aching body…and another very warm body stretched out beside her. With a split-second rush of memory it all came back, and heat spread outwards from her belly to envelop every part of her.

She groaned softly. Thankfully Rafael wasn't holding her any more. She looked at him suspiciously, and couldn't help the kick of her heart at seeing him looking so arrogantly satisfied and relaxed, big limbs sprawled in abandon. The sheet was doing little to mask the evidence of his impressive manhood.

She blushed to remember how she'd encircled him with her hand, and how it had felt to have him thrust into her that first time. In a panic, she scrambled off the bed and stood, breathing heavily, sure he'd wake. But he didn't, although he shifted slightly.

Isobel couldn't believe it. It was as if all her precious intentions and resolutions to do all she could to make this man divorce her had taken a hike last night. She touched her mouth. It felt sensitive and swollen. She cringed now when she thought of how she'd clung to Rafael so desperately afterwards. It must have been like extricating himself from an octopus. And when she'd asked *Is it always like that?* Isobel cringed—he'd turned her brain to complete simpering bimbo mush.

Not even bothering to look for her underwear, she stole out of Rafael's bedroom and back to her own, certain that he wouldn't welcome waking with his wife wrapped around him like a vine.

Isobel could only have been asleep for about ten minutes when she woke again with a start, to see Rafael standing by her bed, naked as the day he was born. Heat drenched her in seconds and she gripped her sheet. 'What is it?'

'What the *hell* do you think you're doing?'

A little of Isobel's fire came back even as she tried to ignore that gorgeous naked body. She felt a rush of liquid heat between her legs. 'I'm sleeping. What does it look like?'

'What are you doing in here? The last thing I remember is you in *my* bed, where you belong.'

His easy dominance made Isobel spit, her recent feelings of vulnerability still far too vivid. 'I wanted to come back to my own bed. I wanted some space.'

Rafael reached down and plucked the cover from Isobel's nerveless fingers, twitched it back to the end of the bed.

She gasped and scrambled for it. 'How dare—?'

But her words were cut off when Rafael all too easily picked her up in his arms. Isobel fought furiously. All the while her body seemed to simultaneously melt and go up in flames. She'd slipped on loose silk pyjama bottoms and a camisole top to sleep in, and they felt paltry now, when Rafael's hot skin was burning through to hers.

He carried her back into his bedroom and unceremoniously dumped her on the bed, where she fell in an ungainly sprawl. She immediately moved to escape to the other side of the bed, but Rafael grabbed her ankle and stopped her. She turned back, breathing heavily, to see Rafael's hand snake higher and higher, over her calf, her knee, her lower thigh…her upper thigh. And suddenly she wasn't fighting any more.

His long, lean, naked and *aroused* body was pressing down

over hers again, and once again she was rendered mute, a slave to this man's touch. She trembled.

'Are you sore?' he asked innocuously.

Isobel shook her head. She wasn't sore. Yes, she ached a little, but there was another ache building, and only one person was capable of assuaging it.

As if he could read her mind, he said throatily, 'Good. Because I think that this time we might be able to make things last a little longer... And, Isobel, I *do not* want to hear the word *space* ever again—*entiendes*?'

He bent his head to one pouting breast and clamped his mouth over one already hard and tight nipple, suckling through the delicate lace of her camisole. The action of his mouth mixed with the wet lace of her cami made Isobel squirm underneath him, groaning softly as all resistance washed away in a wave of heat.

CHAPTER TEN

WHEN Isobel finally woke again, some hours later, she was sprawled across Rafael's bed, a sheet tucked around her. She knew that she was alone. She'd half woken earlier to hear Rafael getting dressed. She felt too lethargic to move, too lethargic to even blush when she thought of how *long* Rafael had made it last that time. How she'd been clawing his back with her nails, begging, pleading for release...

She turned her head face down into the pillow and moaned. Her fears that intimacy would make her feel something for Rafael had been well founded. She was on a roller coaster of emotions and feelings that made her want to cry and laugh at the same time. She resolutely refused to look at the suspicion that these emotions went a lot deeper than simple morning-after fuzziness.

Isobel flipped over on her back and looked up to the ceiling. It *had* to be just the natural feelings that arose from losing your virginity to someone. A natural biological result of sharing intimacy.

The bedroom door opened and Isobel shot up in the bed, clutching the sheet to her, heart thumping. She wasn't ready to see Rafael so soon. But it was Juanita coming into the room, with a tray holding some orange juice. She put it down beside Isobel, who flushed with embarrassment, but Juanita just smiled serenely.

Isobel blinked, and watched as she opened the curtains to let the morning light in. Was this the same woman?

Juanita turned and said jauntily, 'Señor Romero has gone to the office. He said to tell you that I will be moving your belongings into his room today.'

'But—' Isobel started to protest, and then stopped under a baleful look from Juanita. 'Okay,' she said weakly instead, knowing that if she stopped Juanita from carrying out Rafael's autocratic instructions he'd simply do it himself. No wonder Juanita was so pleased. She must feel that Isobel was finally being a good wife to Rafael. But it made Isobel nervous—as though Juanita knew something she didn't.

She didn't even have the strength to let that thought annoy her as much as it should. All she could think of was the night to come, and the ones after that, repeating what she'd just shared with Rafael. In all honesty she didn't think she'd be able to cope.

By the time the weekend was over Isobel felt emotionally wrung out. Rafael filled her—mind, body and soul. They'd only been sleeping together for two nights, but already it was nearly impossible to remember a time when she hadn't slept in the cocoon of his possessive embrace. He was consuming her utterly, and her already tenuous control of her emotions was rapidly unravelling.

So when he informed her coolly over breakfast on Monday morning that he still intended to come with her to see the estate agent about her dance school, she protested. 'Really, you don't have to do this. I know how busy you are...'

He just looked at her. 'I'm coming with you, whether you like it or not, so get your things ready.'

She didn't argue any further, recognising the implacable expression on Rafael's face.

The effect of his presence when they arrived at the building in La Boca was almost comical. The estate agent she'd been photographed with blanched when he saw him, and within mere minutes the price was down so low that Isobel felt guilty.

Within an indecently short space of time she and Rafael were standing in a huge empty room with high ceilings and massive windows. Isobel was a little shell-shocked.

'Don't you like it?' Rafael asked, rocking back on his heels with hands deep in his pockets.

She shook her head quickly. 'I love it. It's just…all happened a bit fast. I'd kind of envisaged this being a slow process.' She shot him a wry smile. 'I think for most mortals it *is* a slow process.'

Isobel saw Rafael's eyes drop to her mouth. It tingled, and Isobel could feel warm colour flood her cheeks. An intense spasm of lust made her belly clench, and down lower she flooded with liquid heat. God, if he was to tip her onto the floor right now and make love to her she knew she wouldn't, *couldn't* object. She didn't move as Rafael prowled towards her with all the threat and grace of an indolent panther.

She lifted her chin helplessly, eyes snared by his. He reached out and hooked a hand to the back of her neck, drawing her towards him slowly and inexorably. He took her right hand and lifted it up. His other hand moved slowly down from her neck to her back as he pulled her into a tango embrace. Through an open window came the faint strains of a waltz from where street performers had set up outside.

'Rafael—' Isobel croaked out, terrified that he *would* try and make love to her and see just how wanton he made her feel.

'Shh.' He halted her protest and started to dance with her.

In flat shoes Isobel had to stand on tiptoe. She couldn't help but sink into his embrace. Rafael's lead was all too easy and seductive to follow. Isobel wasn't sure how long they danced around the empty room, with dust motes floating in the air, to the music of someone else's dance, but when they finally stopped she was breathing hard and felt disorientated. Weak as a kitten. Dancing a tango with Rafael before they'd slept together had been cataclysmic, but dancing it *now*, after having been intimate with him...

Rafael bent his head and feathered a kiss to the corner of Isobel's mouth. 'If you're happy with this place then I'll arrange for everything to be put in motion.'

Isobel was struggling to find her equilibrium, seriously scared at how easily Rafael managed to turn her whole world upside down with just a touch, a dance, a light caress.

She nodded her head, moving back, pushing herself out of his arms. She needed space to think. Right now he could have pointed to a tiny galvanised garden shed and she would probably agree to take it as the studio.

'Yes...that sounds...good.'

He took her by the hand to lead her out of the building, and without his intense focus on her Isobel felt as if she could draw breath again. She was very afraid of confronting what was in her heart now she had little or no reason to hate Rafael any more.

She'd told him that he'd never know *her*, but she hadn't counted on what it would do to her to know *him*.

The following day, as she helped Juanita to move the last of her things into Rafael's room, Isobel saw the housekeeper holding a box.

'What do you want to do with this?'

Isobel recognised the rosewood box she'd taken from the

estancia. She'd forgotten all about it. She explained to Juanita that she'd brought it to try and get someone to open it, so she could see what was inside, and Juanita led Isobel outside to a garage at the side of the house, where Rafael's general handyman was working. Isobel said a shy hello, realising that she hadn't really made an effort to get to know the rest of the staff yet.

Within a few minutes, and with minimal damage to the box, Carlos had it open. Having given him an effusive thank-you, Isobel went back into the house and into her now empty suite of rooms. She sat cross-legged on her stripped bed and opened the box.

In it she found bundles of letters tied together with ribbons. Opening them with shaking hands, she realised that they were love letters. For a heart-stopping moment she thought they were letters from her grandmother to someone other than her grandfather, but then realised that they weren't. They were between her grandparents—both sets of letters, from both sides. Right from when they'd met as teenagers up until they were married.

Carved into the inside of the lid was the inscription *'Together for ever, my love.'* Isobel already had tears threatening before she'd even opened the first letter.

The letters were at first as gentle and loving as she might have expected, but to her utter surprise, as their relationship had become physical—well before their marriage, by all accounts, which had a blush stealing into Isobel's cheeks—they became by turns heated, passionate, cajoling, jealous and sometimes downright X-rated, bringing Isobel vivid memories of her own from the last few nights. It gave her a whole new insight into the rather idealised love she'd imagined her grandparents to have shared.

After closing the box again, Isobel vowed to put it where

it belonged—in her grandparents' burial vault. She felt emotionally strung out at having borne witness to something so intimate and private, and couldn't help the tears spilling over, sliding silently down her cheeks. She angrily brushed them away, but they kept coming, thick and fast. She tried to tell herself it was just grief for the past…but it wasn't, and she couldn't keep fooling herself.

It was grief for the fact that *she'd* never know that kind of requited love.

Lying back on the bed, she had to face up to what was really going on inside her own heart. She was head over in heels in love with Rafael. Everything she'd just read summed up exactly how she felt, and she couldn't deny it any more. It had been there, growing stealthily, since that night he'd first kissed her, when he'd set the bar so high that every other man had fallen far short.

It had been in her unconscious desire to *save* herself for him—as if on some level her body had already known that only he would be able to wring such a sensual response from it. It had been there in the way he'd consumed her utterly since he'd walked back into her life. It was in the way that at every turn he'd proved himself to be the opposite of the man she'd believed him to be, making her see depths and shadows that made him achingly vulnerable even though she knew he'd rather die than show it.

She knew now that she'd been fighting Rafael so desperately not because she'd feared the external prison of a life behind gilded marriage bars, but a much scarier, more internal prison.

Rafael walked into the darkened bedroom and saw Isobel's sleeping form on the bare bed. Hot anger rushed to the surface as he assumed she was going to insist on staying in this room, despite sharing his bed, but then he stopped in his tracks.

He cursed softly when he saw the unmistakable signs that she'd been crying: dried tear tracks like delicate silver trails down her cheeks. A hard knot twisted tight in his chest and he felt momentarily winded.

He saw the rosewood box near her hands and recognised it. Reaching down, without disturbing her, he opened it up and plucked out a letter, flipping it open. As he read his face grew sombre.

Silently he folded it back up and replaced it, straightening just as Isobel stirred and her eyes opened. Rafael saw the way her cheeks leached of colour when she saw him there, and a knot twisted tight in his gut.

'What time is it?' she asked huskily. 'I must have fallen asleep.'

'It's 7:00 p.m.'

Isobel sat up, looking deliciously tousled, her hair standing up on her head. It took all Rafael's strength to not flatten her back down and shut out the clamour of disturbing voices in his head by making love to her. But that was a luxury he couldn't afford right now.

'I thought you were working late?'

'I was meant to be...but I'm afraid I need you for a little damage control.'

Feeling unbearably exposed and sensitive after her afternoon of revelations, not to mention from sitting beside the man who made love to her with such intensity that her whole body quivered like a tightly strung bow just to be near him, Isobel was retreating back to where she felt safe, trying her best to push Rafael away again. Despite knowing how futile her efforts were, because he'd already breached every defence.

He'd explained to her that Bob Caruthers was jittery

after witnessing their dramatic public display the other night; they'd run out without even saying goodbye. Not to mention the fact that he'd also been with them the night Rafael had had to all but carry an inebriated Isobel out of the restaurant.

Mortified, because Isobel now knew what was at stake, she'd said, 'I'm not the only one to blame, Rafael. I'm not the one who initiated a tango display more suited to the back streets of La Boca.'

His mouth had been a grim line. 'I told you that one of the reasons I wanted to get married was to stop public specula- tion and talk. So far we're not doing a very good job of it.'

Isobel's hands had clenched at being reminded of the loveless nature of their union. 'Well, that could be in part because this marriage was never a mutual decision. We were thrown together, thanks to events outside our control.'

As she'd watched him, it had seemed to her for a moment as if some of his golden-olive colour leached from his face. But then he'd turned, fixing her with that black, glittering glare. Isobel's heart had thumped.

'Save it, Isobel,' he'd bitten out. 'Just try to pretend we're in this together tonight.'

Silent for the journey, Isobel felt her head ache.

She let Rafael take her by the hand to lead her into the ex- clusive restaurant. They greeted Bob and Rita, and for the entire evening Isobel drew on every single piece of social training she'd received growing up.

Rafael caught her eye, and Isobel felt a frisson of approval transmitted from him to her. For a moment she basked in a heady sense of pleasure, only to realise later what it meant. She was falling headlong into that world—the world she'd always fought against—and yet she wasn't feeling oppressed.

There wasn't even a hint of wanting to rebel within her. It was giving her immense pleasure to be supporting Rafael.

She was realising this and feeling extremely tender as Rafael followed her into the house when they returned home. She turned abruptly, inarticulate words on her lips, suddenly wanting to talk to this man who felt like a stranger and yet at the same time like someone she'd known for ever. But he put a finger to her lips and then replaced his finger with his mouth, spearing his hands into her short hair, caressing her skull, kissing her senseless.

He pulled away, and it was a struggle for Isobel to open her heavy eyelids. He just looked at her intently. 'Thank you for this evening. Bob Caruthers told me while you were getting your coat that he's going to sign the last contract to let me set up the business here…we did it.'

Relief flowed through Isobel, but it felt as if she was standing on quicksand, knowing that she'd never thought she would be concerned about something like this. 'I'm glad,' she said huskily. 'I'd hate to think I'd played a part in sabotaging something so important.'

Rafael moved closer, bringing Isobel flush against him, and through the thin silk of her dress she could feel his burgeoning arousal. Liquid heat invaded her veins and made her feel wobbly.

'See? We can be good together.'

Isobel's heart was thumping hard. She felt as though she was stepping over a fine line in the sand. One more step and she'd be committed to something untenable—a life half lived with a man who would never love her…and whose love she was beginning to crave with an awful, desperate hunger.

'Maybe…' was all she could say.

'Maybe *nothing*,' he replied harshly, and in the next second Isobel was lifted into his arms and carried upstairs.

* * *

A month later Isobel was feeling dazed from the intensity of the lovemaking Rafael had subjected her to the previous night. She felt as if there was no space in between to grab her breath. Each time they slept together it was more intense than the last, taking another piece of her soul, her heart. Dragging her deep into a dark vortex of bittersweet pleasure mixed with emotional pain.

She was getting ready to greet the guests coming for dinner to the house that evening. Putting gold earrings in her ears, she couldn't believe how much her perception of Rafael had changed; a huge part of his work was pure philanthropy, and the reason it wasn't more well-known was because of his own innate humility. He simply didn't want people to know, believing he got more out of clients and colleagues if his charitable work was done anonymously.

After a last cursory inspection, Isobel left the bedroom to join Rafael downstairs. She steeled herself, locking away her tender secret core in a bid to protect herself from the pain of Rafael's emotional distance. Her heart clenched as she remembered a day just a couple of weeks ago, when he'd surprised her by encouraging her to take the vintage Bugatti out for a drive, despite her protestations.

She'd been terrified and exhilarated in equal measure, and when they'd arrived back at the house she'd been unable to keep the huge grin off her face, believing for a moment that perhaps Rafael was opening up to her. But it had been a mirage.

Within seconds she'd watched as Rafael had visibly closed up in the face of her joy. The afternoon had been ruined, and since then she'd been careful not to read too much into anything, no matter how intense their lovemaking might be. Clearly Rafael didn't and would never feel anything more for her.

In a desperate effort to try and morph into the wife that

Rafael evidently wanted, Isobel had found herself accepting invitations to endless rounds of coffee mornings with her peers, and had been swept up into a whirlwind of shopping on the Avenida Alvear, and trite conversations centring mainly around gossip. She'd even succumbed to a manicure.

It had been a pathetic attempt to see if she could break Rafael out of his cold shell, gain a measure of the approval she'd felt that night they'd had dinner with Bob. She'd only lasted days before Rafael had found her weeping tears of frustration as she tried to get the hideous acrylic nails off with acetone.

He'd taken her raw and red hands to inspect them and she'd sniffed. 'I can't do it, Rafael. I tried, I really did, but I can't do the society thing.'

In a curiously tender moment he'd bent his head and kissed the corners of her mouth reverently. 'It's okay. I don't want you to be like those social vultures. Let's find Juanita. I'm sure in her chequered past she has gained some knowledge of false nail removal.'

That small moment had made Isobel fall even more in love with Rafael, but afterwards it had been as if nothing had happened. He'd gone back to being cool and distant.

Except at night... Then there was no coolness or distance. Only intense heat followed by pain, when Isobel curled up next to his body and recalled that he'd lost his heart a long time ago and never intended losing it again.

Cursing herself for thinking of all this now, she descended the stairs.

Rafael was waiting for Isobel to come downstairs. She had been preparing all day with Juanita for their guests. He frowned minutely. Even Juanita had come under Isobel's spell, and the two were now staunch allies. He poured himself a measure of whisky and drank it back in one gulp, wincing only slightly as it burnt its way down his throat. His marriage was progressing exactly to plan. He had no reason to complain…*and yet it wasn't enough.* Isobel didn't fight him any more. She didn't come at him the way she first had, like a raging tornado of quivering injustice about every little thing.

Now she looked at him warily, and spent most of her time working on plans for the dance studio. She'd retreated to somewhere he couldn't reach. She'd once told him he would never really know her, and he now realised what she'd meant.

He felt unaccountably bleak, frozen inside. And he knew the only thing that alleviated that feeling would be when he held Isobel's panting, naked and trembling body in his arms later that night. His body started to respond to that image, and with a growl of frustration and a clawing feeling of guilt Rafael poured himself another drink.

His mind went back to a few weeks ago, when he'd felt so lighthearted for the first time…*in a long time.* The day he'd encouraged Isobel to take the Bugatti out for a drive. It had only been when they'd got back to the house and she'd turned her shining face to him that he'd realised he'd never seen her so happy. The only other time he could remember a look resembling that had been after their exhilarating horse ride at the *estancia* that day, or when she'd got the keys to her dance studio.

He'd realised then that she must be happy because for a brief second she was the girl in Paris again, with no responsibility or commitment. Even as he'd been thinking that he'd seen the look of pure unmitigated joy slide from her face, and it had been like a cold finger touching his heart, confirming his suspicion that for a moment she'd forgotten herself, but was now remembering that she was all but incarcerated in a marriage she didn't want.

A sound came from the door, and Rafael turned to see the object of his thoughts standing there, looking hesitant. She wore a softly draped silk dress in a dark chocolate colour, exactly like her eyes. Gold hoop earrings drew the eye to that slender neck, and gold strappy sandals made her legs look even more lissom. *She was finally his.* And yet, mocked a voice, she wasn't. That thought nearly felled him.

The breath stuck in Rafael's throat, but he managed to get out, 'You look stunning.'

Isobel made a self-deprecating face, but Rafael couldn't fail to notice the slight shadows under her eyes, and more, in her eyes, making them look even more dark and mysterious. A red-hot skewer lacerated his insides.

Isobel was trying not to be floored by Rafael's sheer gorgeousness in a black suit and white shirt. Trying to ignore the way her heart seemed always to respond to his presence by picking up a more urgent beat.

Her heart was already constricting at seeing him looking so cold and stern. But before she could say anything the first of the guests started to arrive, and Isobel found herself caught up in acting the hostess.

At one point during the evening, when she was making polite but meaningless conversation, she slid a glance to Rafael, who was similarly occupied. She had to reconcile herself to the fact that this was all he really wanted from her; she didn't even have a reason to fight him any more. She'd been wrong about so many things…

The only other thing he would ask from her eventually would be to start a family. Isobel couldn't doubt that. She knew as well as he the importance of heirs. It would be one of the primary requirements of their marriage.

Her belly contracted at the thought of a family with Rafael—a tiny baby with dark, dark eyes and hair. She'd never really contemplated the reality of being a mother, but now she knew that she did not want to bring children into the sterile environment of their marriage. If she had children she wanted them to be surrounded by love and affection and two parents who loved each other. But not to the exclusion of everyone else, which she could see now had been the fatal flaw of her grandparents' love, shutting out her mother and making her hard and cold as a result.

Rafael caught her eye then, and lifted a brow minutely, silently asking her if anything was wrong. Isobel shook her head and smiled a brittle smile, and went back to her conversation. But it was a lie, because everything was wrong, and it was for the very last reason Isobel would have expected. She had no problem living this life. She just couldn't live it in isolation, without her husband's love.

When the final guest had left, Isobel closed the door wearily and bade goodnight to Juanita.

Rafael surprised her by coming out to the hall, holding his car keys. He looked intense. 'I'd like to take you somewhere—would you come with me?'

Isobel frowned. 'You want to go out *now*?'

He nodded slightly. He'd taken off his tie, and just the small glimpse of his powerful chest made Isobel feel weak. Perhaps putting off the sensual torture to come wasn't such a bad idea.

She shrugged nonchalantly. 'Okay.'

Without talking, Rafael helped her into his Range Rover. Feeling more and more bemused, she watched as Buenos Aires went past them and he eventually drove into an area between La Boca and San Telmo. They parked across the road from a crumbling building and Rafael got out, coming round to take Isobel's hand.

He led her across the road and she asked, 'Where are we going?'

The last time Rafael had been spontaneous had been the day he'd let her drive the Bugatti, and the memory of that was bittersweet.

He gestured to the doorway in front of them, partially obscured with thick, heavy, velvet curtains. 'In here.'

As they walked in, Isobel felt the heat of many bodies rush to meet them, and then heard the strains of tango music. It was a *milonga*. They emerged into a huge, brightly lit and ornately decorated room, where what seemed like hundreds of couples were dancing around the dance floor, engrossed in their own little worlds. Her heart clenched hard.

Rafael led Isobel over to a quiet seat at one corner of the dance floor and ordered some drinks. It was only then that he said, 'This *milonga* is where I learnt to tango. It's where my grandmother used to bring us.'

Isobel looked at him. 'You mean you and your brother?'

He nodded, his eyes following the dancers. 'My grandmother knew what was happening…the beatings…so I think it was as much an effort on her part to try and protect us as anything else…'

Isobel's heart literally ached in her chest at being reminded of what had happened to him. She put a hand over his in an unconscious effort to sympathise, knowing words would be superfluous. He looked directly into her eyes, and the intensity of his gaze made Isobel feel dizzy. For a second she could almost imagine—

Mentally she shook her head and broke their gaze, looking out to the dance floor. She *had* to stop this awful yearning.

She took her hand away from his and focused on the dancing couples. There were hundreds of similar halls all around Buenos Aires, filled with anonymous couples who would dance far into the early hours of the morning.

It was a place of respected codes. If a man wanted to dance with a woman he would signal from across the room with his eyes and she would decline or accept as she wished. They would then dance three dances, or more if they were an exclusive couple. This place wasn't for the fainthearted or the beginner. It was for Buenos Aires natives and tango lovers, who came to lose themselves for a few hours in the music of melancholy and a dance of great beauty and sensuality.

So when Rafael stood and held out his hand Isobel was powerless but to accept. She stood and went into his arms, ducking her head, terrified that he might see something of her heart in her eyes.

Going into his arms felt all at once like coming home and being sent to Siberia.

Slowly they started to move. Songs merged into one another. They didn't break apart once. Another song came on, and Isobel lost count of how many tangos they danced. She just knew that she could have stayed like this for ever, with her head tucked into Rafael's jaw, eyes shut, and their bodies so close that she couldn't tell which was her heartbeat and which was his.

It was only after a few moments that Isobel realised that the song playing now was 'Volver,' sung by Carlos Cardel. It was the same song she'd watched her grandparents dance to all those years before, and with each step and each achingly sung word of the song Isobel's composure started to unravel.

Tango was passionate and erotic, but it also encapsulated the depth of human sorrow and loss and pain. The evocative lyrics about returning to a first love finally tore Isobel's heart in two. She stopped dead and pulled herself out of Rafael's arm, tears streaming down her face. She hadn't even realised she'd started crying. He frowned and held out his hand, but Isobel backed away jerkily, away from the dance floor and the other couples still dancing.

'No.' She shook her head. 'No, Rafael. I'm sorry. I can't do this with you. *I can't do this.*'

She turned and all but ran from the hall, out to the empty and quiet street. She started walking towards the main thoroughfare, not even sure where she wanted to go.

She heard steps behind her and felt her arm being grabbed. She was pulled around.

Rafael looked down into her face. 'What is it?'

Isobel dashed tears away with the backs of her hands. They wouldn't stop coming. 'Just what I said, Rafael. I can't do this with you. I'm really sorry. I know how you've come to terms with this marriage of convenience, how you need it for your business, but I never have…I can't.'

Rafael had his hands on her arms now. His voice sounded rough. 'I never wanted to make you this unhappy. But you are, aren't you?'

Isobel nodded dumbly, wishing she had a tissue to wipe her nose. She looked up. Rafael was blurry, but still so gorgeous that her belly tightened even now. She pulled herself free of Rafael, who just let his arms drop.

She took a deep breath. 'I want a divorce, Rafael. If the joint ownership of the *estancia* is an issue I'll sign my half back to you. It's enough that I've seen it again. If I stay in a marriage like this I'll wither and die. And it's not even the marriage itself...if we had love I could cope...but there's no love.'

'No love...' Rafael repeated faintly.

Isobel's tears had finally stopped and she sniffed loudly. 'You teased me once for being a romantic, and I am. That's what's important to me—to live a life with someone I truly love, who loves me. I can't bear the thought of bringing children into a marriage like my parents had...'

Rafael was as still as a statue, just looking at her. And then he said, so quietly that she almost didn't hear, 'You don't love me?'

Isobel felt every self-preserving instinct jump into action. She shook her head. 'You always said this marriage was never about love. Why would I have allowed myself to fall in love with you?'

'Why indeed?'

Isobel couldn't bear to hear another word. She put out a hand. 'Please, can we just go home? Please...?'

Rafael nodded grimly and they walked slowly back to the car. The journey to the house was made in silence, and when they went in Isobel said, without looking at Rafael, 'I'll sleep in one of the spare rooms.'

He said curtly, 'You don't have to do that. I'll take the spare room.'

Isobel shrugged, feeling dead inside, and slowly made her way upstairs, feeling about a hundred years old. She had no idea where they would go from here. All she knew was that she couldn't continue like this, in a vacuum of love.

Rafael stood looking at the space where Isobel had been for a long time. A heavy feeling like a rock made his chest feel tight. It was over. He couldn't do this, either. That was twice now he'd seen her cry. He'd ignored the evidence of her unhappiness, pushed it aside, all in some ruthless attempt to pretend that it could work…and the truth was it couldn't. Not after what she'd just said.

CHAPTER ELEVEN

THE following morning when Juanita bustled into the dining room Isobel tried to hide what she knew must be enormous circles under her eyes. But Juanita was distracted, and simply said, 'Mr Romero told me to tell you that he'd call you later—after he's out of his meeting in New York.'

Isobel blanched and said something incoherent. She'd completely forgotten that Rafael had a two-day business trip to New York. She sagged back in the chair now that she knew he wasn't about to stride through the door and send her brittle composure to the four walls.

Moving on autopilot, Isobel went to the dance studio for the day, consulting with interior decorators and builders, and interviewing potential dance instructors to work alongside her. But her excitement in the project was diluted time and time again when she stored something away to tell Rafael and then realised that she couldn't expect to do that any more. She hadn't yet asked him if he thought they could work out a way for her to keep the dance studio…she hoped that he wouldn't use it against her.

When he rang her on her mobile later she could tell he was distracted. All he said before ringing off was, 'We'll talk when I get home, okay?'

Isobel nodded silently, her throat thick with tears and finally managed a husky, 'Okay.'

His distraction couldn't have said it any better. He was undoubtedly already working on a way to bring about the end of this marriage and move on with his life. And in all honesty she couldn't blame him. He deserved a wife who could be all the *convenient* things he wanted and not expect love, too.

Three days later, Isobel nearly choked on her glass of water when Rafael strode into his study at the house, looking gorgeously dishevelled and unshaven. He'd rung last night to say he'd been delayed, and Isobel hadn't been expecting him till later that evening.

He was looking at her with such intensity she wanted to ask if she had something on her face. She had to uncurl her fingers from the desk, where they'd gone in a reflexive move to hang on to something concrete.

She half gestured. 'I was just checking something on the Internet.'

Rafael inclined his head. 'I'm going to take a shower, and then I'd like you to come somewhere with me to talk—okay?'

Isobel just nodded. So there would be no reprieve. Straight down to business. Sorting things out. Perhaps he'd take her to his solicitor's office?

On tenterhooks, Isobel fought the desire to change out of her jeans and plain white shirt. When Rafael came back downstairs in black trousers and a black top, hair still wet from the shower and clean shaven, her heart threatened to burst out of her chest.

She stood up from behind the desk and went to join him, following as he led her out to the car. Nerves kept Isobel silent, and Rafael seemed similarly preoccupied, an intense expression on his face as he negotiated the early-evening traffic.

To her surprise she realised that Rafael was driving into a small airfield, where a plane sat waiting. Completely nonplussed, Isobel let Rafael lead her over to the small aircraft. He introduced her to the pilot, and after an exchange between the two men that left Isobel none the wiser as to their destination she followed Rafael into the tiny four-seater craft.

She was too bemused even to ask where they were going as the plane took off into the evening sky, as if talking might bring the end that much quicker. She had a moment of déjà vu, remembering watching Paris grow smaller and smaller beneath her on a flight that felt like hundreds of years ago.

She sent Rafael a quick, surreptitious look, but his gaze was fixed firmly out of the other window.

Isobel only realised she'd nodded off, her recent sleepless nights having finally caught up with her, when she felt someone shaking her gently and saying, 'Isobel, wake up. We're about to land.'

Rafael. She opened her eyes.

He was so close that all she'd have to do to kiss him would be to move forward and press her lips to his. In a panic that she might do just that and betray herself, she jerked back, noticing his cheeks flush and his eyes flash.

He sat back down, face stony, and they both did up their seat belts. It was only when the plane straightened to land that Isobel recognised where they were.

She gasped. 'It's the *estancia*.' She looked at Rafael accusingly, her heart tripping at being back here. 'Why have you brought us here?'

Rafael was grim. 'You'll soon see.'

Isobel folded her arms and looked out of the window as the plane touched down. When they'd landed, and the pilot had helped them out, Isobel watched aghast as he proceeded to take off again into the rapidly sinking sun.

She looked around to find Rafael waiting patiently by the open passenger door of a Jeep. With nothing else in sight, she had little choice but to climb in.

Her belly churning, Isobel saw that they weren't actually that far from the house, which she could see in the distance. But when they came out at the long drive, instead of turning left to go to the house, Rafael turned right.

Isobel's nerves were in shreds. 'Where are we going?'

'Not far now.' Rafael took a sharp left turn into what was seemingly a solid bank of bushes, but Isobel could see after a moment that it was actually a hidden dirt track. He drove into the blackness until they came out into a clearing that Isobel could see was near the lake which stood at the back of the house.

He brought the Jeep to a stop and turned the ignition off. The silence was suddenly deafening. He got out and came around to Isobel's side, taking her hand silently, helping her out and onto the soft ground. He looked at her for an intense moment, and then led her farther into the clearing.

Isobel saw lights ahead, and as they came closer she made out a beautifully ornate gazebo almost entirely covered in ivy and flowers. At once her chest tightened and she put a hand up to it. This had to be the gazebo that had been mentioned in some of her grandparents' love letters. This was where they'd first met. Isobel had vowed to look for it when they came back, but had forgotten about it till now.

As they came closer she could see that it glowed with the lights of a thousand small and large lanterns. Isobel turned and looked up at Rafael, taking her hand out of his. For the first time since she'd known him, he looked nervous. 'Rafael… why are we here?'

Finally, he spoke. 'I saw what was in the box that belonged to your grandmother, and I hope you don't mind but I read the letters, too…' His mouth quirked, but the smile didn't reach his eyes. 'They seemed to move you.'

'They did,' Isobel said faintly, remembering that moment when she'd had to face what was in her own heart.

His voice was husky. 'I didn't know what to do…how to do this. I thought maybe a letter…but how could I compete with *their* letters? And it didn't feel right. It's not me.'

Isobel felt as if he was talking another language. 'Rafael…?'

He put a finger up to her mouth. 'Just let me speak, okay? I need to speak.'

Isobel nodded. Rafael took his hand away, but not before trailing that finger down and across her jaw, almost as if he couldn't help touching her. Isobel's heart kicked painfully. Even now she was projecting…

'The other night…I wanted to try and talk to you…so I took you to the *milonga*… I thought that might make it easier. When we dance it seems like we can communicate on another level… But before I could speak you told me exactly how you feel.' He looked at her. 'You need love to go on in this marriage.'

Isobel nodded faintly, barely breathing, spellbound by the intensity in Rafael's gaze. Surely he didn't care so much about maintaining this marriage that he was prepared to go to such theatrical lengths just to make her feel cared for?

And then he said, so quietly that she had to strain to hear, 'But there *is* love, Isobel.'

Rafael touched his chest, and Isobel could see a tremor in his hand.

'There is love—in here. I wanted to tell you the other night, but you were so upset, and then I didn't want to burden you with my feelings when you clearly just wanted to get away from me.'

Isobel couldn't believe what she was hearing. She shook her head. 'But...how? I mean, when...?'

Rafael grimaced and ran a hand through his hair, leaving it dishevelled. 'I think it started when we first met, but I compartmentalised you into my future very neatly. I didn't start to deal with it until I came to get you in Paris. The truth is, you were affecting me way before that. I couldn't even sleep with another woman in the six months before I saw you again. The night I saw Ana beside you...it was like seeing a dull piece of dirt next to a bright shining diamond. That was when I knew I was in trouble—even though I didn't really recognise what was happening. I couldn't fully admit it because whatever I had felt for her was nothing compared to how you made me feel.'

He shook his head. 'I've been falling and falling and trying to convince myself I wasn't...I had to admit it when it tore me apart to know that I was making you so unhappy. I know you want out of this marriage, but I still need to try...to see if there is any chance you will stay if you know what you mean to me.'

Feeling the blood start to rush through her veins with a giddying sweep, Isobel forced herself to stay calm. 'What *do* I mean to you?'

Rafael's jaw tightened, and a muscle throbbed. His voice was gruff. 'Everything. Without you, nothing makes sense.'

He pulled something from his back pocket. It was their pre-nuptial agreement. He ripped it up and threw it on the ground. 'That means nothing without you, because if you were to leave I wouldn't want anything that reminds me of you. The *estancia* is yours—it should have always been yours. My father was determined to lock me into an arranged marriage because he resented me and the fact that my brother had got away. Your grandfather was a convenient pawn to that end.'

Rafael smiled with a tinge of wry sadness. 'I had no idea who you were going to become, or how you'd have the power to force me to my knees.' His smile faded. 'My experience with Ana made me bitter and cynical. I shut down my emotions, couldn't believe I'd let someone fool me into believing I'd fallen in love.' He took a deep breath. 'But it wasn't love at all, because I now know what love really is, and it's standing right in front of me, breaking me apart inside.'

Isobel took a deep breath and picked up Rafael's hand. Everything was silent around them. She looked up at him and felt a deep sense of peace and homecoming wash over her. She placed his hand over her heart and said, 'My heart beats for you, Rafael. I wasn't brave enough to tell you that, though. I told you I needed love, but I needed *your* love, because I already love you.'

Tears started to threaten, and her voice hitched. 'I fought it for so long, and the moment I realised it every second became torture—because I was convinced you'd never love me. You'd lost your heart so long ago, and you'd shut yourself off…that's why I fought against sleeping with you for so long. I knew it was my last defence. On some level I knew I was falling in love with you from the very start.'

Incredulously, Rafael reached out his other hand and pulled Isobel close. *'Tu me quiero?'*

'Si,' Isobel said on an indrawn quivering breath. *'Te quiero mucho.'*

With shaking hands Rafael cradled Isobel's head, spearing his fingers through her hair, tipping her face up to his so reverently that Isobel couldn't help more tears from spilling over. He bent his head and kissed her once, twice, and then for a long, long time, as if they'd never kissed before.

Isobel could taste the salt of her tears, and when Rafael finally pulled away he wiped his thumbs over her wet cheeks.

'That's the last time I want to see you cry…' he said gruffly.

Isobel smiled a watery smile. Her mouth felt plump and swollen, and she just wanted Rafael to kiss her and keep kissing her for ever.

But just then a sound came from nearby, and they both looked around to where the housekeeper was making an apologetic face as she righted a fallen lantern in the gazebo. Isobel could see that there were at least two other people there, too, but she couldn't make out who.

Isobel looked up at Rafael questioningly. 'What's going on?'

He smiled, and Isobel's heart ached when she could see that he still looked nervous. 'This is why I brought you here.'

He got down on one knee before her. He took her hands and said, 'I want you to know that if I'd been able to choose you for myself I would have brought you here, to this place. And I would have got down on one knee and asked you to marry me— not because of a years-old marriage pact, but because I love you and you love me. So, Isobel Miller, will you marry me, here tonight, and make me happier than I ever thought possible?'

Isobel looked up at the night sky for a moment, to try and stem the tears flowing thick and fast. But it was impossible. So she looked back down at her husband and cried and smiled and nodded, and finally managed to get out a choked, 'Yes, I'd like to marry you very much.'

Rafael stood and led Isobel into the small candlelit gazebo, where she could now see the housekeeper standing beside Miguel Cortez, who looked after the polo horses, and a priest.

There, in front of their two witnesses, they were married again in a heart-achingly simple ceremony by the local priest—who afterwards got onto his bike and followed them back to the *estancia*, where the celebrations went on until the early hours of the morning.

Four years later, the Isobel Romero Dance Studio, La Boca

'Look, it's Papa!'

Rafael winced and mouthed *sorry* to Isobel as her dance class was effectively disrupted for a moment as their three-year-old daughter broke free of the orderly line and threw herself into Rafael's arms, where he stood at the door.

Rafael caught Beatriz up and kissed her soundly, making her giggle, and then he shut the glass door so that Isobel could get on with the class.

Beatriz put her hands on Rafael's face so that he looked at her, her little face lit up with joy, brown eyes sparkling. 'Papa, I felt the baby kick just now—really hard. He's going to be coming soon.'

Rafael quirked an amused brow. 'Oh? So you think it's going to be a *he*?'

'Silly Papa. Of course he's going to be a he. We already have a girl—*me*.'

Rafael smiled and figured he couldn't argue with that logic. He hugged his daughter close, all the while keeping a protective and loving eye on his beautiful, glowing and heavily pregnant wife. She sent him a dry look through the door, and he sent one right back that said, *Look all you want. I'm not going anywhere*. She sometimes protested that he was too overprotective, but Rafael wasn't about to have it any other way.

And one month later Beatriz's prediction came true—her baby brother Luis was born…

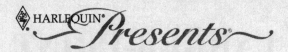

Coming Next Month

from **Harlequin Presents®** EXTRA. Available October 12, 2010.

#121 POWERFUL GREEK, HOUSEKEEPER WIFE
Robyn Donald
The Greek Tycoons

#122 THE GOOD GREEK WIFE?
Kate Walker
The Greek Tycoons

#123 BOARDROOM RIVALS, BEDROOM FIREWORKS!
Kimberly Lang
Back in His Bed

#124 UNFINISHED BUSINESS WITH THE DUKE
Heidi Rice
Back in His Bed

Coming Next Month

from **Harlequin Presents®**. Available October 26, 2010.

#2951 THE PREGNANCY SHOCK
Lynne Graham
The Drakos Baby

#2952 SOPHIE AND THE SCORCHING SICILIAN
Kim Lawrence
The Balfour Brides

#2953 FALCO: THE DARK GUARDIAN
Sandra Marton
The Orsini Brothers

#2954 CHOSEN BY THE SHEIKH
Kim Lawrence and Lynn Raye Harris

#2955 THE SABBIDES SECRET BABY
Jacqueline Baird

#2956 CASTELLANO'S MISTRESS OF REVENGE
Melanie Milburne

LARGER-PRINT
BOOKS!

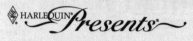

GET 2 FREE LARGER-PRINT
NOVELS PLUS 2 FREE GIFTS!

YES! Please send me 2 FREE LARGER-PRINT Harlequin Presents® novels and my 2 FREE gifts (gifts are worth about $10). After receiving them, if I don't wish to receive any more books, I can return the shipping statement marked "cancel". If I don't cancel, I will receive 6 brand-new novels every month and be billed just $4.55 per book in the U.S. or $5.24 per book in Canada. That's a saving of at least 13% off the cover price! It's quite a bargain! Shipping and handling is just 50¢ per book.* I understand that accepting the 2 free books and gifts places me under no obligation to buy anything. I can always return a shipment and cancel at any time. Even if I never buy another book, the two free books and gifts are mine to keep forever.

176/376 HDN E5NG

Name	(PLEASE PRINT)	
Address		Apt. #
City	State/Prov.	Zip/Postal Code

Signature (if under 18, a parent or guardian must sign)

Mail to the **Harlequin Reader Service:**
IN U.S.A.: P.O. Box 1867, Buffalo, NY 14240-1867
IN CANADA: P.O. Box 609, Fort Erie, Ontario L2A 5X3

Not valid for current subscribers to Harlequin Presents Larger-Print books.

**Are you a subscriber to Harlequin Presents books
and want to receive the larger-print edition?
Call 1-800-873-8635 today!**

* Terms and prices subject to change without notice. Prices do not include applicable taxes. Sales tax applicable in N.Y. Canadian residents will be charged applicable provincial taxes and GST. Offer not valid in Quebec. This offer is limited to one order per household. All orders subject to approval. Credit or debit balances in a customer's account(s) may be offset by any other outstanding balance owed by or to the customer. Please allow 4 to 6 weeks for delivery. Offer available while quantities last.

Your Privacy: Harlequin Books is committed to protecting your privacy. Our Privacy Policy is available online at www.eHarlequin.com or upon request from the Reader Service. From time to time we make our lists of customers available to reputable third parties who may have a product or service of interest to you. If you would prefer we not share your name and address, please check here. ☐

Help us get it right—We strive for accurate, respectful and relevant communications. To clarify or modify your communication preferences, visit us at www.ReaderService.com/consumerschoice.

HPLP10R

HARLEQUIN®

A Romance

FOR EVERY MOOD™

Spotlight on

Inspirational

Wholesome romances
that touch the heart and soul.

See the next page
to enjoy a sneak peek from
the Love Inspired® Suspense
inspirational series.

See below for a sneak peek from
our inspirational line, Love Inspired® Suspense

Enjoy this heart-stopping excerpt from
RUNNING BLIND
by top author Shirlee McCoy,
available November 2010!

The mission trip to Mexico was supposed to be an
adventure. But the thrill turns sour when Jenna Dougherty
and her roommate Magdalena are kidnapped.

"It's okay. I'm here to help." The voice was as deep as the darkness, but Jenna Dougherty didn't believe the lie. She could do nothing but lie still as hands slid down her arms, felt the rope around her wrists.

"I'm going to use a knife to cut you free, Jenna. Hold still."

The cold blade of a knife pressed close to her head before her gag fell away.

"I—" she started, but her mouth was dry, and she could do nothing but suck in air.

"Shhh. Whatever needs to be said can be said when we're out of here." Nick spoke quietly, his hand gentle on her cheek. There and gone as he sliced through the ropes on her wrists and ankles.

He pulled her upright. "Come on. We may be on borrowed time."

"I can't leave my friend," Jenna rasped out.

"There's no one here. Just us."

"She has to be here." Jenna took a step away.

"There's no one here. Let's go before that changes."

"It's dark. Maybe if we find a light…"

"What did you say?"

"We need to turn on the light. I can't leave until I know that—"

"What can you see, Jenna?"

"Nothing."

"No shadows? No light?"

"No."

"It's broad daylight. There's light spilling in from the window I climbed in through. You can't see it?"

She went cold at his words.

"I can't see anything."

"You've got a nasty bruise on your forehead. Maybe that has something to do with it." His fingers traced the tender flesh on her forehead.

"It doesn't matter *how* it happened. I'm blind!"

Can Nick help Jenna find her friend or will chasing this trail have Jenna running blindly again into danger?

Find out in RUNNING BLIND, available in November 2010 only from Love Inspired Suspense.